The Rancher's Secret Love

The Rancher's Secret Love

A Montana McGregor Brothers Romance

Paula Altenburg

TULE
PUBLISHING

Dear Reader,

Thank you for visiting Grand, Montana! It sits where the Tongue and Yellowstone rivers meet, not quite two hours from Billings.

The McGregors are descendants of a pair of dark-haired, green-eyed, wild Irish brothers who came to Montana from the Old Country intent on making their fortunes. They followed the army, selling them goods (you can correctly interpret that as contraband) until they found the perfect place to call home. They built Grand with great expectations. The Wagging Tongue Ranch has been home to McGregors for six generations now.

Jake, Luke, and Zack McGregor view themselves as caretakers, preserving the ranch for future generations. They're currently bringing the family business into the twenty-first century. They can't preserve a family business, however—or future generations, for that matter—if they don't settle down.

This is Luke's story. Luke is the scholar. He's the sensitive McGregor, the one easiest hurt, and the brother without a real goal in life. That is, until he meets Mara.

I hope you love Mara—and Grand!—as much as Luke does.

Chapter One

L UKE MCGREGOR EYEBALLED the freshly painted pink walls.

His mother had converted the former nursery into a sewing room twenty-five years ago, after the youngest McGregor graduated to a big boy bedroom. Now her sons were converting it back.

Fat pink blobs of paint speckled the drop cloth Luke and his brother Zack, the big boy in question, had spread to protect the honey-colored hardwood floor. The sewing machine, plus their mother's sewing supplies—the reams of fabric, the hundreds of buttons, the dozens of spools of thread—had been boxed up and donated to the local ladies' auxiliary.

Luke swallowed around the lump in his throat. Cleaning out this room was the hardest thing he'd ever done. It really drove home the fact that she wasn't coming back.

"Wow," Zack said, his gaze sweeping the small room. A fine spray of pink from the roller he'd used on the ceiling dusted the deep reddish-brown of his hair. "That's really pink."

"Yep. Just like the boss ordered," Luke said.

He tapped the lid closed on the paint can with the wooden tip of his brush. He had no quarrel with pink. His issue was with their older brother Jake's automatic assumption that all little girls loved the color when there had to be at least a thousand alternatives to choose from. Or so it had seemed when he checked out the paint chips at the hardware store in Grand.

But Lydia Williams—their twenty-month-old niece—was likely too young to care what color her new room would be, and Luke's judginess about it might be because he disliked Jake making all the decisions. It was an ongoing theme in their thirty-one year relationship.

And his biggest issue likely wasn't even with Jake. A lot of shit had gone south in Luke's life of late and Jake made a good target for his pent-up aggression. Luke had to force himself sometimes to remember that his brothers had both suffered big losses, too. Three family members were gone. Four, if he counted their brother-in-law, Blair. The hole they left inside him was enormous.

But Denise showing up, pretending to care, and then walking away when he needed her most, was the worst kind of betrayal, and he wasn't sure he'd ever recover from that.

"Now's not the time to talk about marriage. I'm okay with you being in Montana for a few weeks to help your brother get the kids settled in," she'd said, cool as could be. *"But I'm not okay with you giving up a prime teaching position that you worked hard for so you can stay an indefinite amount of time. And I'm certainly not staying here with you. I'm truly sorry for your loss, but this isn't our problem. The ranch and the kids*

belong to your brother. Our life is in Seattle."

Luke had thought it was, too. Right up until he'd gotten the phone call that his parents, his sister, and his brother-in-law had all died in a plane crash in Peru. The trip had been a birthday gift from Liz and Blair to their father. Liam McGregor had talked for years of his desire to see Machu Picchu someday.

The dream had turned into a nightmare. One the McGregors would have to deal with as a family, because Luke had discovered his hard-earned, incredibly rare teaching position at the college wasn't nearly as important to him as the people he loved.

He loved Denise, too. Or at least the woman he'd believed her to be. It was possible he didn't know her as well as he'd thought, because he couldn't wrap his head around her refusal to stand by him right now. In his experience, it was what people who loved each other did.

Instead, she'd boarded her flight to Seattle without once looking back, leaving Luke to question his values and what was important to him, something he'd never had to consider before.

"We could add a wallpaper border," Zack said.

"What?" Luke had lost the thread of their conversation.

"A border. You know—with teddy bears, or dolls, or something." Zack stretched his neck muscles, rolling his shoulders. "Maybe Disney princesses. Little girls love that crap."

No way was Luke supporting gender stereotypes. Let Lydia grow up to be a free thinker. She was a human being with a mind of her own. "Maybe we should wait and see what she likes rather than stick her with something she might end up hating."

"It's a nursery, not a prison cell. When she's old enough to have her own room, she'll be able to tell us how she wants it to look." Zack examined the wall. His blue eyes, the same shade as their mother's, held a frown. "But until then, we should do something to offset all this pink. It looks like the inside of a wad of cotton candy in here. It's making me nauseous."

"Everything makes you nauseous."

Zack's weak stomach was a family joke that dated back to a long car ride to Nevada when they were kids. But in this instance, Luke couldn't say he was wrong.

The paint was really, really pink.

Rooms for ten-year-old Mac and five-year-old Finn had been easier to prepare. Luke had taken pictures of their man caves in New York and he and Zack had recreated them here as best they could.

Lydia, however, still shared her parents' bedroom, so they'd had nothing to guide them. He and Zack knew squat about little girls and even less about babies. Their sister, Liz, had been the eldest McGregor sibling, and growing up, she'd fit right in with the boys.

Guilt punched Luke in the gut. He'd been so obsessed with earning his PhD and landing a teaching position, he'd neglected spending time with his niece and nephews. Other than the funeral, he'd last seen them for a few days at Christmas five months ago. Visiting them once a year wasn't enough to form a solid relationship with them and things were about to change. They deserved the happy childhood their mother had planned for them, and now, it was up to her brothers to make it happen.

But putting Jake in charge… What had Liz been thinking?

Jake was the responsible McGregor, yes. No arguing that. He wasn't the fun uncle, however. Not by any stretch of the imagination. Luke and Zack had to step up or those poor kids were doomed.

"We don't have enough time," Luke said. "We can't put a border on until the paint is set, and Jake and the kids should be here sometime tomorrow."

Jake was driving from New York City to Grand, Montana rather than flying, as he'd planned. Something about Finn having a meltdown at the airport—which came as no real surprise. Finn was five and he'd just lost his parents and grandparents in a plane crash. Reasoning with him wouldn't have been an option.

Bet that threw Jake.

"Maybe it will look better once the furniture's in place," Zack said, focused on the paint, but the expression on his face disagreed with the hope in his tone.

"There's only one way to tell." But Luke didn't think it would, either.

They stripped the tape from the trim and the fixtures, then spent the next hour assembling a practical white crib and matching change table. Luke spun the last screw, then the brothers righted the table and set it across the room from the crib. Shoulder to shoulder, arms folded, they studied their handiwork.

"Want to talk about it?" Zack asked.

"What's there to talk about? The walls are still pink," Luke replied.

"That's not what I meant."

Luke avoided looking Zack's way, not wanting his pity. "I know what you meant. The answer is no."

Denise had left three days ago, right after they'd agreed their long-term goals were no longer in sync. There wasn't much more to say about it that Zack couldn't figure out for himself. He'd been there. Besides, it wasn't as if Luke's crushed life dreams were the worst thing that had happened in this family of late.

"If you change your mind, I'm here for you," Zack said.

Luke had to get out of the house. He needed some time alone. He loved his brother, but the guy was crossing personal boundaries. Since when did they discuss feelings?

"It's my turn to buy groceries, isn't it?" he asked.

Zack got the message. "Yeah. Can you add fennel to the list? I found a focaccia recipe I want to try for supper tonight."

Luke had no idea what fennel was, or focaccia either, for that matter, but he wasn't asking for clarification. Zack liked to cook, and if given the chance, he could launch into long explanations.

Now Luke understood how first-year computer science students felt when he rambled on about code.

He tilted his wrist. His sleeve rode up his arm to reveal

the gleaming, rose-toned, diamond-studded, stainless-steel watch his parents had given him when he'd received his PhD last September. He had a little over an hour before his shift in the dairy barn began. Even though his relationship with Jake could often be tense, the eldest McGregor brother had enough on his plate and Luke wouldn't add to his worries.

When Jake arrived home with the kids, he'd find everything at the Wagging Tongue Ranch in order.

MARA RAMOS SPOTTED the newcomer the minute he walked through the automatic sliding glass doors.

He was so very pretty, no one could miss him.

She'd traveled the world for many of her twenty-six years, and spent almost two of them as a dancer for one of the hottest new names in pop music—the bastard—so she was no stranger to good-looking men. In her experience, men this pretty turned out to be gay.

Her radar was good though, and the newcomer, despite the fluid, elegant lines of his movements, didn't give off that vibe. So maybe pretty wasn't quite the right word for him.

But neither was handsome.

He was tall, at least six feet, likely more. Thick brown hair that nudged the edges of black hung a little long in the front. It flipped over a pair of eyes so green she could identify the color from three aisles away. He wore a white cotton shirt with the sleeves rolled up and the collar unbuttoned. The tails dangled, untucked. He had long, muscled legs wrapped in a pair of skinny, hipster jeans that screamed this was no cowboy. Untanned, smooth-skinned, long-fingered hands confirmed the disclaimer. He wasn't used to manual labor.

He had the look of an academic.

Mara, who'd grown accustomed to the plethora of tempting cowboys in Grand, was intrigued by this outlier. He strolled through the glass doors as if he'd done so his entire life, clearly at home here, and yet, there was no way he belonged. She worked her way closer, pretending to check out the baking supplies next to the spices, where he'd come to a halt.

Concentration—or maybe confusion—pinched his eyebrows together.

"Can I help you find something?" she asked.

Mr. Pretty glanced her way, but his gaze didn't linger. He went right back to perusing the spices, his attention fully engaged in his mission.

"Any idea what fennel is?" he muttered, more to the shelves than to her.

Mara didn't consider herself vain, but if she were, she'd now be disabused.

"Yes, but it depends on what you need it for," she replied. "You'll find fennel seed here, but if you want it fresh, you should check out the produce aisle."

"I need it for focaccia," he said. "And, no, I don't know what that is, either."

The last comment was delivered with an upraised eyebrow and a hint of self-deprecating humor. Green eyes—*so, so pretty*—swiveled toward her. Not even a flutter of interest marred the cut of those gems. Maybe he was married. She checked his left hand. No ring, but fine dots of pink paint freckled the backs of his fingers.

Mentally, Mara examined the evidence. He'd been painting. He was shopping for ingredients she could only assume someone else would be using to cook, since he had no idea what he was doing.

What a shame. He wasn't single.

While she wasn't interested in forming a lasting relationship with any one particular man, a temporary diversion would have been welcome. Grand was a small town, its sources of entertainment restricted, and the nights could be lonely and long. Cowboys, however, tended to be a tad too possessive when it came to the women they slept with and she liked her freedom. It made it so much easier to move on when the time came.

"Focaccia is a type of bread. If that's what the fennel is for, then I recommend fennel seed. You sprinkle it on top of the dough and drizzle it with olive oil before you bake it." She reached around Mr. Pretty, plucked a small jar off the shelf, and handed it to him. "Here you go."

"Thanks."

Nope. Not even a teensy bit of interest.

She was about to move along and finish her own shopping when Diana O'Sullivan, pretty as a picture, rounded the corner and entered the aisle, a six-month-old in a baby carrier strapped to her chest. She pushed a loaded grocery cart with a three-year-old boy riding shotgun in it. Her eyes widened with pleasure when she spotted Mara.

And then Mara realized Diana was focused on Mr. Pretty, not her.

"Luke McGregor," Diana exclaimed. She hurried toward them. "I was so, so sorry to hear about what happened to your parents and Liz. How are you all holding up? How's Jake?"

"Jake's being his usual hardheaded, competent self," Mr. Pretty replied. "He's supposed to arrive home with the kids sometime tomorrow." He ruffled the hair of the wide-eyed, somber child in the shopping cart. "Hey, Marcus."

Mara taught dance lessons in Grand so she heard her share of its gossip. The pieces fell into place. Mr. Pretty, potential underwear model, in reality was Dr. McGregor, local boy genius. He taught computer science at a college in Seattle.

She began edging away, intent on minding her own business. Even if Dr. McGregor turned out to be single, he was no more her type than a cowboy would be. She was no scholar. Not even close.

He was also grieving, meaning he most likely had issues. She could do without those.

"Hi, Mara," Diana said, acknowledging her presence with a radiant smile that cut off Mara's escape. "Sorry to interrupt. I didn't realize you and Luke knew each other."

"We don't," Mara said. "He was looking for fennel."

"Zack's making focaccia for supper," Luke added.

Zack being the third McGregor brother, so Luke wasn't grocery shopping on behalf of a girlfriend or wife, which changed nothing. The McGregors had suffered a tragedy, and even without the life lessons she'd learned about needy men, Mara wasn't so crass as to intrude on his grief.

"Mara is Grand's one and only dance teacher. She gives Zumba classes, too." Diana jiggled the restless baby strapped to her chest. "She used to be a dancer for Little Zee. You can see her in his video 'Hot Like This.'"

Mara died a little inside. Dr. Pretty, with his PhD in computer science, wasn't about to be any more impressed by that than he should be. He wouldn't even know who Little Zee was.

And as for Little Zee—whose real name was Jim—he'd dropped Mara on her second day in the hospital after she broke her leg on a skiing trip in Big Sky. She'd still been in traction.

Sorry, babe. I've got to replace you.

That was the last she'd seen of him. It had taken her a full week to figure out that he hadn't only meant professionally. He'd had all of her belongings shipped to her parents' home in Brazil. How thoughtful—considering Mara was stranded in Montana. Then she'd learned on *TMZ* that he'd begun dating an actress.

Had the actress heard all about the faithless high school sweetheart who'd given up on him because he was living out of his van and street performing in subways? Who hadn't believed in him enough to stick it out until he found success?

Or maybe he'd turned Mara into the heartless diva of his latest personal drama. Little Zee's acting was even better than his music, and in truth, his music wasn't half bad.

"Wow. I've heard the song on the radio, but I've never seen the video. I'll have to check it out," Luke said politely, sounding about as impressed as she'd expected. He held up the bottle of fennel seeds and gave them a shake. "Thanks for the help, Mara." He kissed Diana on the cheek. "It was great seeing you, Di. I've got to run, but drop by the ranch with the kids anytime. Bring O'Sullivan, too."

He strode off, calm and in no apparent great hurry, but he didn't fool Mara. He'd avoided speaking about his family and their recent loss, neatly turning the conversation, then he'd ducked out at the first opportunity. The biggest tell, however, was that he'd lost the easy form to his movements that had first caught her eye.

"Poor Luke," Diana murmured, half to herself. Pity pooled beneath her black lashes, suggesting she wasn't fooled by him, either. She patted the baby nestled against her and spoke to Mara, fixing her smile back in place. "How are things at the studio?"

"Great."

Mara's stomach clenched around the lie. Thankfully, Diana was too nice to call her on it. Why bother when they both knew the truth?

A dance studio in Grand was akin to offering ice skating lessons in Honolulu. The only way Mara could keep up with the bills without dipping too deep into her savings was by offering steep discounts to parents looking for cheap ways to occupy their children for a few hours on Saturday mornings. And, of course, the adult Zumba classes.

She probably should have opened up shop in Billings or

Missoula, but in the cities, she would have faced more competition. Her original plan was to establish her reputation in Grand before moving on. She was only twenty-six. There was no rush. She'd needed this past year to pull her life back together and Grand had been kind.

But she hadn't expected the locals' complete indifference to her qualifications, which included ballet and jazz at some of the best schools in the world, not to mention two runs in Broadway musicals before her agent convinced her to give pop videos a shot. People seemed to think being pretty was the only skill she'd required to get where she'd been.

Her damaged leg was all the proof she'd needed that being pretty wasn't nearly enough. For her, beauty was about movement. About rhythm and grace. It had been almost a year and a half since the accident now, yet her leg continued to ache and her knee still gave out without warning. She didn't give a damn about the Dr. Frankenstein scars. Her passion was dance. She'd be happy to be able to demonstrate a decent pirouette to her young students. She'd lost an important piece of herself and she wasn't going to recapture it anytime soon.

The baby began to fuss. One pudgy fist grabbed the front of her mother's sleeveless cotton blouse.

"Has the landlord fixed the lock on the studio door yet?" Diana probed, ignoring the squirming bundle.

"He said he'd get to it later this week."

The landlord was in his nineties, the crime rate in Grand wasn't high, and only a few people knew the lock was broken, so Mara chose not to stress about it. The rent was cheap and she wasn't rocking the boat when she could brace a chair under the doorknob. The result was the same. She'd lived in far worse conditions.

Diana, however, who was one of the nicest people Mara had ever met, didn't share her lack of concern. A troubled frown replaced her smile. "I'll send Randy over to fix it tonight."

This was one of the things Mara did like about Grand, and why she'd decided to start her dance studio here. She liked the sense of community. People were happy to step in and help out, and while she'd learned that cowboys could be territorial when it came to the women they dated, there'd be no obligation at all in accepting anything from Diana and Randall O'Sullivan. He was as nice as his wife.

There was no point in arguing. Nothing to be gained. She'd only offend them.

"Thank you," she said.

Dr. Pretty had finished his shopping. He carried his small bag of goods through the sliding glass doors and into the sunny parking lot outside. His elegant ease of movement had returned—and with interest. He aimed for a four-door, dark blue economy car.

Mara couldn't say what she'd expected a professor with grassroots deep in Montana to drive, but that wasn't it. Or maybe she was thrown because it wasn't a half-ton truck, which was what everyone else around here seemed to own, no matter what their occupation.

She dragged her attention away from Dr. Pretty to discover Diana had her phone out and was texting her husband.

"He says to expect him around eight," Diana announced.

Chapter Two

M ARA'S STUDIO OVERLOOKED Sutler Cemetery, its name a proud nod to Grand's history. It had a nicer ring to it than Bootlegger Burial Ground, which from the stories she'd heard, would have been the more accurate tribute.

The historic pioneer cemetery was beautiful, no matter what it was called. Ancient cottonwood trees draped the wrought iron fence that enclosed it. Two worn gray stone pillars, with fine surface cracks sprouting green moss, supported the front gate. Inside, gravel pathways wound between well-tended grave markers dating back two hundred years and brilliant white hydrangea bushes. Only founding family members could be buried here anymore, but it was a lovely, peaceful place to go for an early morning stroll before the day's temperatures soared.

When she got home, a familiar, four-door, dark blue economy car huddled in the shade of the cemetery's small parking lot that her studio shared.

For a second Mara puzzled over why Luke McGregor was here when he'd left the store in such a hurry, but then she remembered the McGregors were one of Grand's founding families, and his parents' remains had already been interred, even though the memorial service wasn't scheduled until the upcoming weekend.

He emerged from between the stone pillars as she was lifting the grocery bags out of the trunk of her little red hatchback. Sunshine draped his shoulders. He hesitated, as if he didn't know whether to continue onward or retreat into the shadows of the cottonwoods.

She pretended not to see him, allowing him the privacy he so obviously wanted. She guessed Dr. Pretty wasn't holding it together as well as he'd like Grand to believe and she could sympathize with that.

She set the bags on the asphalt, slammed the trunk closed, then slipped her palms through the canvas straps, dividing the load between her two hands. She straightened, went to take a step, and as she did, a wave of white-hot, blinding pain shot from her shin to her thigh.

Her bad knee gave out. Her groceries hit the ground seconds before she sprawled into an inglorious heap of scattered cans and fresh produce. A jar of organic peanut butter rolled under her car. Her long hair saved one elbow, which got tangled in it.

Footsteps pounded on the pavement, drawing closer, before she could collect herself. She clenched her eyes closed in mortification.

"Hey." A smooth, masculine voice, oozing concern, floated a few inches above the back of her head. "Mind if I help?"

The question turned out to be more of a warning that he

intended to touch her rather than a request for permission, because he didn't wait for an answer. Strong, warm hands grasped her arms.

She opened her eyes. Emerald-green irises glittered behind black-framed lenses, so close to her face she could see the tiny flecks of gold surrounding each pupil. And a suspicious hint of red rimming his eyelids.

He helped her get her feet under her. Once she was upright his eyes dropped lower, assessing the damage. They halted, and narrowed. "You okay?"

The leg of her Capri pants had hitched up, exposing her mangled knee.

A hot blush straddled her cheeks. She hated pity. No one understood that a few scars weren't important to her. Her dancer's feet were ugly, too. She had corns on the joints of each toe, bunions that hurt if she wore tight shoes, and the two toenails she'd lost had grown in thick and deformed. None of that stopped her from wearing sandals.

Because she didn't care how they looked as long as they worked. Beauty of movement was everything to her, and she'd just face-planted with all the grace of an albatross, a harsh reminder that she'd never dance professionally again.

But she'd give up her good leg before she'd give in to self-pity, and she wouldn't tolerate it from others. She'd dance again—just not professionally.

She gathered her hair in both hands, looping it into a bundle, and shoved it over her shoulder and away from her face. The action bought her a few seconds.

"I'm fine. It happens sometimes." There was no point in

pretending her leg wasn't the reason she'd fallen. Dr. Pretty was smart. "Thank you," she added, not wanting him to think she wasn't grateful.

"Let me help you with these."

He stooped and began to gather her scattered purchases, dropping a packet of cellophane-wrapped baby spinach into one of the canvas totes. Mara spotted the jar of peanut butter under her car at the same moment he did.

His lips settled into a straight line and his eyebrows rode up in a cool challenge. The look he shot her said, *"Don't even think about it."*

He dropped to one knee, groped behind the tire, and withdrew the jar. A smudge of dirt streaked the crisp white cuff of his rolled-up shirtsleeve. Dark hair fell forward over his eyes. He flipped it aside. The peanut butter disappeared into one of the totes.

Her left elbow—the one her thick padding of hair hadn't rescued—stung. A quick peek showed she had road rash oozing blood through the tight, three-quarter sleeve of her lightweight knit top. The heels of both palms were scraped too, and the leg of the Capris covering her good knee was suspiciously damp.

"Thank you so much. I've got it from here," Mara said, moving to take the bags from him.

He stepped away, putting them a few inches out of her reach. "No problem. I'll carry them for you."

She began to see the cowboy in him. Luke McGregor, however, didn't give quite the same raw, he-man impression. He leaned a bit more to the refined, gentleman side—just far enough to intrigue her.

He looked around. "Where am I carrying them to?"

"I live above the dance studio."

He stared at the former warehouse, still sheathed in steel siding that was pockmarked with rust, as if she had to be kidding him. "That's old Angus McKillop's oxygen cylinder filling station."

Defensiveness kicked in at his tone. It didn't look like much, fair enough, but it was her home. "Not anymore. Now it's a dance studio. There's an apartment upstairs."

The apartment used to be office space and ran the length of the building. She'd dipped into her savings to make it a cozy haven where she could relax. Plus, she liked the privacy and the convenience of the studio's location. Downtown Grand was only a few minutes away, and if not for her bad leg, she could walk. From upstairs she had an excellent view of the Yellowstone River. It widened at Grand, its delta fed by the Tongue River, and was rampant with trout sports fishermen, especially in the spring.

They crossed the cul-de-sac between the studio and the communal parking lot. Luke hung back to allow her to open the door of her building. She turned the knob and nudged the door with her shoulder because it tended to stick in the heat. Summer this year was going to be fierce.

She began to have second thoughts about allowing a stranger into her space, but this was Grand and Diana liked him.

Besides, it was too late. He was already in.

The interior was dark, the air cool. It smelled a bit funky, kind of sweaty and damp, like the combination of warehouse and dance studio it was. She fumbled for the light switch.

The glare of a long line of fluorescent fixtures flooded the room. She'd had a double barre installed, as well as a sound system, and a rubber subflooring with a Marley overlay that was perfect for dance. Mirrors lined the wall at the far end of the room. To their left, as they walked in, a flight of prefab aluminum steps, complete with guardrails, climbed fifteen feet to a catwalk that overlooked the studio floor.

"You should lock your door," Luke said.

He sounded so disapproving. She couldn't help yanking his chain. "Diana's husband is coming over to fix the lock tonight."

Luke looked at her. Really looked. As if for the very first time. Then, he blinked.

And she could literally see where his thoughts took him.

"Show me where to put these bags. I'll fix it for you and save Randy the trouble," he said. It wasn't quite a demand, but it was close.

She wasn't fooled by it, either. He was offering to fix the lock as a favor to Diana, not her. As if she were some sort of *femme fatale*. And as if Randy, who so plainly adored his adorable wife, would ever wander.

She plastered on a wide, innocent smile and yanked a bit harder. "Randy doesn't mind."

Luke didn't rise to the bait. Neither, however, did he back down. "I'm fairly certain he won't mind if I fix it for him either, especially since I'm already here. He works long hours trucking and doesn't see a whole lot of his wife and babies."

Making her the unreasonable one if she refused his offer.

Since she didn't care if the lock was fixed or not, and hadn't asked for anyone's help in the first place, he could go right ahead and give it a try. "Thank you for both of us, then. I'm sure there's a toolbox around here somewhere. Mr. McKillop left a few things he thought I might need."

"Sure. So you can handle any maintenance yourself." That faint trace of dry humor he'd exhibited earlier reemerged. "McKillop claims to be Irish, but there's a lot of Scottish in him."

She couldn't help smiling, because Mr. McKillop did, indeed, make a big deal out of being Irish, but she wasn't about to get sidetracked by another interesting facet to Dr. Pretty. She was looking for a distraction, not a cause, and she'd already determined he had too many issues. Her romance with Little Zee wouldn't be forgotten anytime soon.

"You can check in the utility room under the stairs to see if there's anything you can use. I'll put the groceries away," she said.

Luke didn't relinquish the canvas totes. "I'll carry them up the stairs for you first."

Dr. Pretty's roots were really starting to show. "If you insist."

She led the way, secretly relieved he was doing the heavy lifting. The aluminum stairs, which gave her the sensation of walking on manhole covers and tended to tremble, were a challenge for her at the best of times, and although she'd gotten used to carrying things to her apartment, right now her knee ached something fierce.

"Your elbow is bleeding," Luke said from behind her.

She glanced back, careful to keep a firm grip on the rails, to where he'd halted a few steps below her. Concern radiated from the perfect lines of his face.

His eyes were so distractingly *green*.

She'd almost think he wore colored lenses, except Dr. Pretty was also pretty masculine, and he didn't strike her as all that invested in his appearance. He was trendy, perhaps. The haircut testified to that. But he hadn't noticed the dirt on his sleeve—or if he had, he didn't care. His style likely had more to do with his career choice than any personal preference.

"It's just a scrape. I'll clean it with hydrogen peroxide and put a Band-Aid on it," she said. She kept a first aid kit in the studio for her dancers, but a smaller one in her personal bathroom for her own use.

They reached the catwalk. She hesitated at the steel door that led to her kitchen. While she was okay with a stranger coming into the studio, she wasn't as okay with bringing one into her private living space.

Luke must have sensed it, or perhaps all that gray matter he owned told him it wasn't a smart move on her part and he shouldn't help her commit an act of stupidity. He propped the bags against the wall. "I'll go see what I can do with that door."

He strode the short length of catwalk to the stairs. She really did like the way he moved. He had some of that inherent cowboy swagger, but with an added touch—his body flowed, every muscle connected, a lot like the way water rippled over rock. Disappointment that they wouldn't be getting to know each other better settled in.

What a shame their situations weren't better aligned. He would have made a good... dance partner.

LUKE CLATTERED DOWN the rickety stairs, the noise of his shoes on the aluminum risers amplified by the cavern's acoustics until it echoed through the steel beams overhead.

He hadn't paid much attention to Mara when she'd spoken to him in the grocery store. He'd had too much else on his mind. Besides, his breakup with Denise was far too fresh for him to take notice of other women, no matter how pretty they were.

He hadn't expected to see Mara again, either. Especially not here, right next door to the cemetery. All he'd wanted was a few minutes alone with his parents. To check out their graves before the memorial service so he wouldn't break down in front of Grand, his brothers, and the children. It was doubtful Mara had noticed he'd shed a few tears. That was a nasty tumble she'd taken.

He wondered what she'd done to her leg, because no way dancing had done that type of damage.

He found the toolbox in the storage room where she'd thought it might be. Fixing her door meant he'd be late getting back to the ranch, but he couldn't imagine Diana being okay with her husband doing it. Mara was a young, stunningly beautiful woman and Randy wasn't dead.

Luke didn't know what old man McKillop was thinking either, because no matter what her age or appearance, a woman living alone should have a door she could lock.

He examined the main entry to the warehouse. The latch wasn't catching, but the knob seemed to work. He'd have to take the door off, adjust the hinges, and rehang it. The strike plate on the frame needed to be widened, too. He could file that down easily enough. He was looking at an hour for the entire operation.

Well, it couldn't be helped. Jake's hired hand could keep an eye on things in the barn until he arrived.

He snagged his phone from his back pocket and called Zack. "Hey. I'll be a few minutes late. I'm doing Diana a favor."

Zack's voice crackled back, the reception distorted, most likely thanks to the decrepit steel siding on a building dating back to Grand's pioneer days. "Whatever. Did you get my fennel?"

Luke made a rude comment as to what Zack could do with his fennel as confirmation. The signal dropped before Zack could rebut and he tucked his phone away, grinning to himself over how it had to be killing Zack not to get in the last word.

He caught sight of Mara descending the stairs and his grin faded away.

She'd changed her clothes. Now she wore a pink T-shirt—the color appeared to be trending—and a long, flowing, multi-hued skirt that swirled alarmingly around her ankles and couldn't possibly be safe on that mobile contraption. Her flat sandals appeared practical, at least. Thick, chocolate-brown hair licked with highlights of toffee swung between her shoulders. A patch of white gauze covered an elbow.

She reached the warehouse floor without any mishaps and Luke let out the breath he'd been holding. He was going to speak to McKillop's son, Ian, about the condition this building was in and ask him to convince his tightwad father to fork over the money to make some repairs.

She crossed the floor toward him, almost as if she were floating. The slight limp took nothing away from the dancer's grace of her movements. Cool blue eyes, so striking against the warm, honeyed hue of her skin, settled on him.

"How is your fixing my door doing Diana a favor?" she asked.

Damn. She'd overheard.

She was maybe five feet five inches, at least eight inches shorter than he was, and she had to look up when she spoke to maintain eye contact, but she'd managed to make him feel six inches tall. He scrambled to come up with an explanation she might believe.

"Do you have any brothers?" he asked.

Two finely-shaped eyebrows went up. Meanwhile her eyes narrowed, ever so slightly. "No."

"Trust me, if you did, you wouldn't want one of them up in your business, either. You'd lie to them, too. It was a lot easier than trying to explain how I ended up fixing a door for a beautiful woman I only just met."

He'd thrown in the compliment for good measure, but it was sincere. Mara—he didn't even know her last name—was an eye-catching blend of Latina, and judging by her blue eyes and high-boned features, northern European.

Denise's face flashed into his head. They'd parted ways barely three days ago, and already here he was, admiring another woman.

Heat churned in his stomach. He'd wanted what his parents had. The closeness. The private jokes. The way they'd looked at each other when they thought no one was paying attention. He would never have had that with Denise. He knew it. Had likely always known it. Her coming to Montana and leaving again had proven as much. He felt a lot of anger, maybe a wee flare of relief because going back to Seattle was one less problem he'd have to deal with, but not one iota of heartbreak. Maybe he wasn't cut out for permanent relationships.

Mara was unimpressed by the compliment. She no doubt received better ones from men every day. "I'm not sure how you ended up fixing it either, yet here you are."

He'd started to reach for a screwdriver in the upper tray of the toolbox on the floor by his foot. The sarcasm made him pause and glance up. She was genuinely angry with him.

He straightened. "I thought you could use a helping hand."

"You aren't helping me. You're helping Diana." Her gaze touched his face. "Either way, it's not your problem. You were right. The landlord should fix it. Leave it for now and

I'll talk to Mr. McKillop."

She wasn't angry. Hurt shone in her eyes.

A lot of things had gone wrong in Luke's life of late. He couldn't blame a single one of them on Mara—who had her own problems, if her living conditions and damaged leg were any indication—so why was he being a jerk to her? Because she was a beautiful woman?

Or because he'd noticed she was?

"I apologize if I gave the impression I don't believe you and Diana's husband can be trusted alone together," he said, wishing he didn't sound so much like his brother Jake—as if he had a giant stick up his butt.

"You don't know me, so I understand. But you do know the O'Sullivans, which means you should know better. Randy's a gentleman."

"True on both counts," he conceded. "I really would like to fix your door, though. It might not make any difference to you, but I'd sleep better tonight."

Mara's face was as expressive as it was stunning. Indecision flashed across it as if it were text in a book, and for the first time in days, an urge to laugh threatened. There'd be no misunderstandings with a woman like this.

The urge to laugh died. It wasn't as if he'd proven to be so great at reading women, so he shouldn't jump to any conclusions about that.

"Thank you, Dr. Pretty," she said. "Yes, I would like the door fixed. How can I help?"

Chapter Three

"D̲R̲. *PRETTY*?" H̲E̲ could think of no better rebuttal.

Her face turned the same shade of pink as her shirt. "Whoops. That just sort of slipped out. I had a doctor in the UK with that name and you look alike."

She was a terrible liar, but since Luke was in no position to cast stones, he let it slide. He didn't know that he cared for being thought of as "Dr. Pretty," though. In junior high he'd constantly been referred to by the teachers as that "cute little kid in 7C."

He'd been a cute little kid, alright. One with an older brother who'd taught him to lead with his left, because he'd had to fight his way through his first half of the school year. By Christmas holidays he'd grown six inches and the black eyes he'd handed out had dwindled to the occasional bloody nose. And also by then, the teachers had discovered he was smart, too.

"Have you ever hung a door before?" he asked.

Again, the expression on her face answered for her. It also warned him she was about to pretend that she had because she couldn't tell he was joking.

"*Aleja de mi a los hombres machistas,*" she muttered under

her breath. *Spare me from macho men.*

He struggled to hold back his grin. That was much better. "I'm kidding. I'm good."

She dragged one of the high-backed wooden chairs that lined a wall—he assumed they were for parents waiting for children—so she could watch while he worked. He hadn't done this type of manual labor since leaving the Wagging Tongue Ranch for college thirteen years ago, and performance anxiety became an issue, but thankfully, like riding a bike, it came back, and he settled in. There was a lot to be said for working with his hands and he'd missed it.

When he was finished, he opened and closed the freshly rehung door. It latched like a dream, if he did say so himself.

Mara abandoned her station and came to stand next to him, admiring his work. She smelled nice. Like mock orange.

"Let me pay you," she said.

Hell hadn't yet frozen over, at least not to his knowledge. "What—I look like some kind of tinker to you? You keep your money, *bailarina.*"

"A *tinker,* hmm?" She tossed her long hair, dropped one hand to her hip, and considered him with sass, beginning to pick up on his sense of humor. Then, she fired back. "No. You don't look like that. *Gracias, vejestorio.*"

The corners of his mouth trembled again. She'd called him an old geezer. Well, he'd been acting like one. And as for what she thought he looked like… He already knew the answer to that.

Pretty. Just how a man wanted a woman to think of him.

He should really be going. He was already late.

"Where did you learn Spanish?" he asked, instead. She had an accent he couldn't quite place.

A bright smile lit the area around her, as if she'd been caught in a spotlight on center stage, sweeping him up in its glow and knocking him off his feet. Not much wonder she'd been featured in music videos. She had charisma.

"You noticed that, did you? We spoke a combination of Spanish and Dutch at home. My father's business took him all over the world, but we spent a lot of time in Central and South America."

"Drug dealer?" Luke deadpanned, because he'd really like another shot of her smile, and got his reward.

"Close. He works in the oil and gas industry."

He couldn't stop being nosy. "So, one of your parents is Dutch, then?"

"My mother. My father is Mexican."

"Which makes you…" Exotic. Unexpected. Far too attractive.

"American. I was born in Los Angeles."

He was well beyond nosy now, and yet, he persisted. "Grand must have come as quite a culture shock."

"I like it here." A hint of sensuality slid into her smile. "More and more all the time."

The purpose of their prolonged conversation finally struck him. They were flirting.

Guilt quickly stripped away any pleasure. He'd ended a relationship with the woman he'd planned to marry only three days ago. He'd promised Jake, who was arriving home tomorrow with three orphaned children, that he'd take care of things at the ranch. The memorial service for his parents had yet to be endured—he and Zack were still cleaning their belongings out of the house—yet here he was. Having a good time, as if he hadn't a care in the world.

"I've got to go." Bewilderment flooded Mara's magnificent blue eyes at the abrupt change in his tone and he tried again. "There's a lot of work to do around the ranch with my brother Jake being away." She'd made him forget about it.

She made him forget a lot of things.

"If you won't let me pay you for fixing my door, then why don't you at least let me take you out for coffee as thanks for helping"—her cheeks colored again—"with my groceries?"

Luke wasn't going to lie to himself. He was tempted. When he was an undergrad, if a woman like this had asked him out, he would have accepted without hesitation and thanked his lucky stars. That was before he met Denise, however, who was pretty and smart, and whose academic goals had aligned so completely with his. She'd also been five years older, with her future already mapped out, and he'd found that especially impressive since he'd had no idea where life after grad school would take him.

The timing was bad. Really, really bad.

But the way Mara fumbled over the reference to her fall was pretty cute. He also liked that she hadn't offered any condolences over the "tragic loss your family has sustained," as one neighbor had politely put it. He was so sick of hearing those words, or anything similar to them. She knew—she'd heard Diana ask him about it—but she minded her own business. In Grand, that was rare.

Plus, despite the blow a damaged leg must have dealt to a professional dancer, and the questionable place she called home—he'd be speaking to the McKillops about that—Mara vibrated with life. She made him think of fire. She glowed, like the lick of flame on a red candle.

He reached for the handle on the now fully functioning door. He'd like to think he was the kind of man who could resist temptation.

"Why don't I call you?" he hedged.

The tiny touch of regret in her smile said she knew that he wouldn't, but she'd play along.

"You do that," she replied.

THE CHURCH BASEMENT was packed tight with people, white-clothed tables laden with food, and an air of festivity that seemed out of place, and yet oddly, came as a welcome relief.

Luke stood close to the cafeteria-style window of the kitchen at the farthest end of the room from the stairs. His tie was too tight, and other than Liz and Blair's New York funeral, the last time he'd worn a suit was to a colleague's wedding last spring. He had Finn, his five-year-old nephew, by the hand. Mac, who was ten, stood beside him. Zack was working the room. They'd left Lydia at home with the teenaged girlfriend of one of the ranch hands.

Jake, the poor bastard, had his back pressed against one

of the round white concrete pillars with no means of escape. He had to bear the brunt of the condolences because he was the oldest and people knew him the best.

Luke had always been the McGregor who didn't really belong. Everyone in Grand had taken it for granted that ranching wasn't for him and he'd be moving on, so that was what he'd done. He didn't regret his education or career. He simply didn't recall ever actively making the decisions himself.

Maybe that was why Lydia's pink bedroom bugged him so much.

And maybe that was why he couldn't shake off his disappointment in Denise. She'd been the push behind his decision to remain in Seattle, and yet, when he'd asked her to move to Montana because it was something he had to do, she'd been opposed. She'd known today was the memorial service and she hadn't called, either.

He knew in his heart they were done, and yet, his heart didn't feel broken. A little numb, maybe. He wasn't exactly sure how he felt about anything, these days.

Finn was having a hard time standing still. He grabbed Luke's wrist in both hands and began to hang from his arm, knees bent and face tilted skyward. Red hair stuck up in the front. Wide, green, trademark McGregor eyes glared at him through a fringe of thick, dark red lashes.

"I want to go home," Finn announced loudly. He'd lost a tooth and he poked his tongue at Luke through the gap.

"Shut up and quit being a baby," Mac said, scowling at his younger brother.

"We don't tell people to shut up," Luke intervened, using his quiet, *I-mean-business*, professor voice that terrified first-year undergrads.

Mac, however, wasn't an undergrad, and he didn't scare easily. "If I don't tell him to shut up, how is he supposed to know he needs to?"

The question sounded so reasonable Luke was almost inclined to cede him the point.

Almost.

"I want my mom," Finn cut in. The pressure on Luke's arm and shoulder increased as he added more weight and a few extra bounces.

"Shut *up*," Mac said again, with added fierceness.

Mac was proving to be an uncanny amount like his uncle Jake. He didn't know how to express his grief, so he took the "be a man about it" approach. Luke found that a lot more troubling than Finn being a kid.

Heads turned their way. Pity was thick in the air. Luke was at a loss as to how to deal with the situation. He could well imagine what everyone was thinking—that the McGregors didn't know how to look after three orphaned kids.

They could think what they liked. Luke had spotted a far greater danger. Weldon Scott, owner of the Running River property next to the Wagging Tongue Ranch, was weaving his way through the horde of people and appeared to be headed Jake's way.

Jake didn't need that. Not today. He'd been holding up fine, but everyone had their limits.

"Finn's behaved himself all day. He's tired and he's bored," Luke said to Mac. "I bet you are, too. We can't go home just yet, but you and Finn can load up plates with whatever you like from the tables and take them into one of those rooms." One side of the basement had been partitioned and turned into rooms for Sunday school classes. "There are boxes of toys for Finn to play with. If you'd rather leave him by himself, that's fine. I'll keep an eye on him." Finn couldn't escape the church basement without someone noticing, and his uncles had all learned how important it was to know what he was up to. His impulse control ranked around zero.

This time, Luke's professor voice did the trick. Mac took his little brother by the hand and dragged him away. Finn, for his part, went willingly enough. Since Luke had just given them permission to load up on cookies and cake, something Jake would not have allowed, why would the boys protest?

Luke could guess who'd be assigned bedtime duties tonight.

He checked on Weldon's progress across the room. Stopping to talk to some of Grand's more prominent residents had slowed him down, but he was narrowing in on his prey. Luke couldn't say for certain that he'd be so bold as to bring up buying the Wagging Tongue from Jake right here and now, but Luke wouldn't put it past him. Weldon might be Diana O'Sullivan's father, but she'd gotten her sweetness from her mother's side of the family. Her father was all about business.

Luke cut around a pillar and quietly squeezed past a group of his mother's friends who were too busy admiring how well Jake was holding up with all the added responsibilities to take notice of him. He stepped in front of the Wagging Tongue's neighbor.

"Weldon," he said.

"Well, Luke McGregor. Or should I say, Dr. McGregor? It's been a long time." The two men shook hands.

Weldon Scott was a big man, solid, but his muscle was slowly melting into soft thanks to advancing age. He had to be pushing seventy. He had a thick head of gray hair and a thin little black line of a mustache that came as a surprise when compared to the single, heavy, salt-and-pepper eyebrow separating his forehead from the rest of his face. He had the tanned and weathered complexion of a man who'd spent most of his life outdoors.

Weldon Scott and Liam McGregor, Luke's father, had never been friends, but they'd always been friendly enough neighbors. The Wagging Tongue controlled most of the water in the Badlands behind the two ranches thanks to a McGregor forefather who'd had the foresight to install the irrigation system that currently supplied the beef cattle wandering the range. Liam had never had any problems with the Running River Ranch making use of it, although the agreement was clear that his permission did not give the Running River any rights.

Weldon wanted the right. He'd happily go deep into debt to buy the Wagging Tongue outright. If he couldn't do that, then he'd go after the rights to the water. And he'd strike at Jake's weakest moment, because overall, Jake was as tough as their dad had been, so this was his chance.

"It has, indeed," Luke replied.

"I'm sorry for your loss," Weldon said. "Your parents were good people and Liz was always such a nice girl."

Luke said something—thanks, maybe—and forced himself to exhale so his lungs wouldn't pop like overinflated balloons. He'd never get used to this. Never. And he prayed the McGregors never had to go through this kind of loss again. Family was everything. He'd never appreciated that more than he did right now.

They discussed the weather, the economy, Luke's job in Seattle, and in general, got the pleasantries out of the way.

"What do you boys plan to do with the ranch?" Weldon finally asked. He was studying Luke the way a professional poker player would, searching for tells. Weldon wasn't a particularly likeable man, but he was direct and he was honest, which was why he and Luke's dad had never had any real trouble between them.

"The Wagging Tongue belongs to Jake," Luke replied. "He'll carry on business as usual."

"My understanding is that you're all shareholders. He and your daddy acquired some significant debt over the last couple of years, though." Weldon looked suitably sympathetic. "That's a lot of business responsibility for three boys to undertake without any experience."

Luke didn't know where Weldon got his information, except he was tight with the manager of Grand's largest bank, so that might be his source. There was also the fact that people in Grand had no qualms about discussing other people's business in public where anyone could overhear. This right here was an excellent example. It wouldn't be long before the topic of this particular conversation spread throughout town.

Not that it mattered. The ranch was Jake's.

"You seem to have more understanding of the situation than me."

Weldon clapped him on the shoulder and left his hand there. Luke had to fight not to shrug it off. Only one man owned that particular fatherly privilege and that man was dead.

"I have a lot more experience behind me, is all. Plus, I knew your daddy when he was in diapers. He'd never cut any of his sons out of the ranch." Weldon withdrew his hand. "If you boys decide you want to sell the place and cut your losses, let me know first. And if you decide you'd like to part with your shares to help pay down the debt before you head back to Seattle, I'd be happy to help you out."

Exactly how deep in debt was the ranch?

The Wagging Tongue ran a combined beef and a dairy operation. The brand-spanking-new anaerobic digestion biomass power plant his dad and Jake had installed wouldn't have been cheap. Neither would the equally new robotic milking system—that Luke was 100 percent behind—have been.

He was about to go collect the boys and call it a day—people had finally begun to leave, so he didn't mind using Finn as an excuse to do so, himself—when a flash of long dark hair snagged his eye. His heart jumped a little, suddenly lighter.

What was Mara doing here?

He shifted course, intent on finding out, but the crowd was thinning and it only took a few steps for him to realize it wasn't her. He should be relieved, and yet, that wasn't the direction his thoughts chose to take. The small bubble of anticipation in his gut developed a slow leak before collapsing entirely.

It had been almost a week since he'd met her and she'd crossed his mind often enough to make him suspect he wasn't the kind of man who could resist temptation, after all.

He had to ask himself why he was trying so hard to resist. He was a free man. Today had clinched that. If the past few weeks had taught him anything, it was that life was short and plans could go sideways in the blink of an eye—something Mara, who'd had to modify her career goals too, could understand. They had that much in common.

He was attracted. She was, too. And best of all, she'd never stick around a dull place like Grand for longer than it took to get her life back in order, so there'd be no strings attached.

She looked like fun.

What was the harm in giving her a call? To find out what else they might have in common?

———∾∾———

MARA HADN'T EXPECTED to see Dr. Pretty again. At least,

not up close. Not after two weeks of silence.

And she definitely hadn't expected him to make good on his promise to call—or to ask her out, either.

It was a Tuesday night, which worked well for her because she taught classes on weekends and weekday afternoons, plus Wednesday and Thursday nights. The sun had just waved goodbye and twilight was settling in. He'd pulled up to the door of the warehouse rather than park on the street or in the parking lot, which was both sweet and annoying. She could walk.

"How's the door working?" he asked when she opened it.

Light from the building thrust the evening shadows behind him. She'd thought her memory might have exaggerated how attractive he was, and how green his eyes were, but no, it turned out her memory was fine. He was tall, his chest broad, and he looked more like a cowboy than he had the other day, but not enough like one yet to fit in.

He'd told her to dress casual. He wore a navy tee under a checkered shirt, a pair of cargo shorts, and canvas shoes. She'd chosen a white, button-down shirt over skinny jeans with rips at the knees. Since high heels were out of the question, at least for the foreseeable future, and she wanted to go a bit girly, she'd grabbed a pair of flat sandals decked out with silver sequins, instead. She'd pulled her hair into a loose, twisted bun at the nape of her neck and secured the heavy mass with about a thousand hairpins.

She swung the door to and fro and peered at the hinges. "Seems to be fine."

"And the lock?"

You don't date much do you, Dr. Pretty?

"It works fine, too. See?" She closed the door and locked it, leaving him on the outside. "Go on. Try to break in. See for yourself."

When he figured out that she wasn't going to open the door for him again—granted, it took him a minute—he actually laughed.

Then, he knocked. "May I come in?"

"That depends. Who is it?" she asked.

"As if I'm going to admit to being a crazed ax murderer."

Thank God she hadn't imagined his sense of humor, either. His IQ might be high, but there had been a growing possibility his emotional intelligence barely bordered on average.

"It's lucky for you I happen to be a very trusting soul." She opened the door.

The night was dry and warm, the shadows still. The town lights blinked on, section by section, behind him. He was smiling, his eyes amused, and… wow. That took away all of the pretty and left nothing but gorgeous. He should smile twenty-four seven.

"Let's start the evening over. You look beautiful," he said. "I probably should have led with that."

"'Hello' would have been an equally acceptable greeting, but thank you. Would you like to come in?"

"Yes, but I made a reservation for nine and we're going to be late if we don't hurry. Maybe later?"

If the reservation was for nine and they were going to be late, then it wasn't in Grand. She wished he'd told her they were going for dinner. She'd assumed a movie or drinks, maybe darts or pool at the local pub, and had already eaten. She would have worn a different outfit, too.

She hadn't quite made up her mind about asking him in at the end of the evening, however. Luke had a lot going on in his life, and that waved a red flag, but he also intrigued her. He'd made it clear the other day he wasn't interested in a relationship—which was a plus as far as she was concerned, because she wasn't, either—yet, here he was. His past weeks in Grand could hardly have been fun and he was probably due for a little.

So was she. The year she'd spent rebuilding her life had been stressful. A year from now, she had no idea where she might be.

Now to find out if they were both on the same page.

She picked up her purse, which she'd brought downstairs with her when the doorbell rang, and tucked it under her arm. She smiled at him, making her interest as plain as she could without being too bold. "That depends on how the rest of the evening goes."

Read into that what you will, Dr. Pretty.

Chapter Four

L UKE INSISTED ON opening the car door for her.
Mara wouldn't have thought twice about opening it
for herself, but the gesture definitely earned him some
points. It was a small courtesy that Little Zee—she couldn't
think of him as Jim because she didn't know who Jim was—
had never bothered to extend.

They turned left at the traffic lights in Grand, then took
the ramp to the I-94 toward Billings, following the twists
and turns of the Yellowstone River.

Luke wasn't much of a talker, but it was an easy silence,
not strained, and Mara didn't mind a man of few words as
long as the words, when he spoke them, were honest.

"Where are we going?" she asked.

"Before I tell you, promise me you'll try it once before
you make up your mind."

She might have some physical limitations at the moment,
but she was game for anything Dr. Pretty could dream up.
Maybe he'd booked a hotel room and had an entire seduc-
tion planned. That would explain why they were leaving
Grand—to keep people from talking.

But Luke didn't strike her as the kind of man who'd

make such a presumption on a first date. He had too much gentleman in him.

That didn't mean gentlemen were necessarily dull—not that she had a whole lot of experience with any. She'd wasted far too much of her life on men who weren't worth the expense.

"I should have warned you," she said. "There are two things I won't try. No mechanical bulls and I'm not into cults. Oh. There's one more," she added. "I'm against human sacrifice—although that one depends on the human, so it's not a deal breaker."

Luke kept his hands at ten and two, and his eyes on the road, but the corner of his mouth levitated. "Good to know you have standards. I'm not going to say human sacrifice is completely off the table, but it's not in my top ten."

"What would make the top ten list of a computer scientist's fun things to do?" Mara mused. She stretched her legs to get comfortable and wiggled her toes under the dash. "Dungeons and Dragons? A Magic tournament? Are we going to a comic book store?"

He cut her a glance and tried to sound stern. "I'm disappointed by your profiling attempts, Ms. Ramos. Shame on you."

"You asked me a lot of questions about my family. Why don't you tell me a bit about yours?" She realized what she'd just said, and how he must feel, and tried to backpedal without making a big deal out of it. "Or, we can talk about something else."

"I still have family," Luke said. "Two brothers—one older, one younger—two nephews, five and ten, and a niece who'll be two in the fall, plus a bunch of aunts and uncles, and a grandmother who lives in a nursing home in Nevada."

He sounded fine, but had a stranglehold on the steering wheel in a way that had her heart going out. Since he really wasn't okay with talking about his family, she'd keep things light.

"You're the brains in the family. So which brother got the looks?" she asked.

"That would be Zack. He's the youngest." The grip on the wheel loosened a little.

"Leaving Jake as the oldest, and the one with the personality." She nodded her head as if she had it all figured out, even though she hadn't met either one of his brothers. If Zack was better looking than Luke, however, then the ladies in Grand should watch out. "Don't worry. Lots of women find intelligence attractive in a man."

"What a relief." He glanced her way again. "Do you?"

The flare of heat in his eyes, carefully banked, and the way those thick black lashes lowered, had her nerves jittering in anticipation.

Nope. This gentleman wasn't going to be dull.

"Yes," she said. "I find it very attractive."

They left the I-94 at the city of Forsyth, situated in a river valley that hugged the banks of the Yellowstone. Luke drove into the city center as if he knew the place well, which of course he likely did, because he'd grown up in the area. It was hard for her to remember, sometimes.

They parked in a small lot between two tall, square brick

buildings. Neither one was a hotel. On the street, they turned toward the building to the right. The sign above the door read, Reality Bytes. Luke held the door open for her to enter first.

"What is this place?" Mara asked.

"You'll figure it out."

There were no mechanical bulls, only a reception counter with a teenager reading a comic book sitting behind it, a few scattered sofas and potted plants, and flashing screens on the black-painted walls. The teen looked up from his comic.

"You must be our nine o'clock," he said, hopping off his stool and coming around the end of the counter with two headsets and a pair of controllers in one hand. "McGregor? Welcome to Reality Bytes. I'm Mike. Follow me and I'll get you started."

"I thought I told you no cults?" Mara said to Luke.

He placed a warm palm between her shoulders and nudged her along. "You're the one who agreed to give it a chance. I, however, didn't make any promises."

They followed the teenager down a dimly-lit, cave-like hall lined with black curtains. Mike pulled one of the curtains aside. "This is your room."

The room had one sofa and a chair. But it was the giant screen on the wall that finally gave it away.

"We're going to play virtual reality games?" Mara asked, angling her head so she could look at Luke, who was standing behind her.

"You okay with it?" he asked.

Was she *okay* with it?

"I've been dying to try this *forever*," she exclaimed, bouncing on her toes with excitement. "Is there a roller coaster?"

Luke grinned, seeming pleased by her reaction.

"Yes," Mike said, answering for him. "We've also got some role-playing games for two people. There's a main menu on the game controller, or we've got a catalog you can look through." He pointed to a magazine on the chair. "I'll give you a demonstration, then once you know what to expect, I'll leave you alone. Press this button here"—he showed them a red LED dot on the wall—"and I'll come help if you need me." He looked at Luke. "You've played before?"

Luke nodded.

Mike gave them a quick rundown of the buttons on the controllers, then passed them the headsets and showed Mara how to put hers on. He tightened the strap for her and adjusted the visor. Mara could hear him, but with the headset and visor, she could no longer see anything but a control panel in the center of the room.

"Follow my instructions," Mike said. "Push the top button on the control panel." The panel vanished and she found herself in a familiar lobby, complete with the art deco gold ceiling, gleaming floors, facing a mural depicting the building. "Good. Now step into the elevator on your right. You're going to the top of the Empire State Building."

She took a few faltering steps forward. God, this felt real. She hoped her leg wouldn't give out. Falling flat on her face in a virtual game would be far worse than taking a dive in a parking lot.

She made it into the elevator. The door slid closed, then the elevator was in motion. It zoomed upward and she swayed. A hand touched her elbow.

"Steady," Luke murmured. "I'm right here beside you. I can see the same things you're seeing on the wall screen. The trick is to remember where your feet are."

She focused on the feel of his hand. On the strength of his fingers. Their warmth made her shiver inside. Then, she felt the floor under her feet and reality returned. So did her confidence. Her bad leg threw her balance off, but a dancer knew her own body.

"I'm good," she assured him.

The touch was withdrawn. The elevator slowed and she stepped through the open doors to the eighty-sixth floor, and more confident now, entered the one to the top. When the doors slid open again, instead of the observation deck on the one hundred and second floor, she found herself staring at a narrow walkway and wide, open sky.

"Step out of the elevator," Mike said.

"You've lost your mind," Mara replied. "I'm not going out there."

Mike, the sadist, had clearly dealt with reluctance before. "Just take one step."

Mara, conscious that Luke, with his PhD in computer science and unhampered grip on reality, was watching her, summoned her courage. She eased one foot onto the walkway, then dragged the other on board.

"You're doing great. Now, walk to the end of the plank."

This isn't real.

When she made it to the end, she couldn't help voicing her pride. "I did it."

"Yes, you did. But you still have to come back down and the elevators aren't working. You have to jump," Mike said.

She'd take his word for it. It wasn't as if she was turning around to try the elevator again, anyway. But she'd naively assumed once she reached the top, that was it. Game over. She stared at the rooftops below her, and at the sky above and around, and considered her options. She could remove her headset and give up. She could close her eyes and hope for the best. She could pass out.

Instead, she focused on her feet. Did anyone die playing these games?

This isn't real. This isn't real. This isn't real.

She jumped.

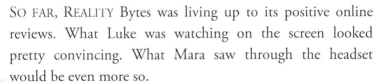

SO FAR, REALITY Bytes was living up to its positive online reviews. What Luke was watching on the screen looked pretty convincing. What Mara saw through the headset would be even more so.

So, when she jumped, he was impressed.

He was also right there beside her in case she took another nosedive. He hadn't forgotten about her leg when he booked the room. He simply hadn't given enough consideration as to the challenge some of the games that required balance might present for her.

The look on her face when she entered free fall, however, seconds before her brain caught up with the illusion, was priceless, and when she removed the headset, her eyes were shining. A few stray locks of brown hair had worked free of the knot she'd bundled it in. His fingers itched to tuck them in place.

"That was amazing!" she cried.

Poor Mike, the kid who'd walked her through her first 3D experience, had gotten completely caught up in her excitement if the silly grin on his face was any indication. It likely matched the one on his own, because Mara incited that sort of reaction. The blue-eyed Dutch features, combined with all of the Latina *vitalidad*, were a tough combination for any male to resist.

They'd been busy getting the kids settled in and ready to start their new school, so he'd had to wait a few weeks to call her, but she was exactly what he needed tonight. The McGregors had met with the ranch's lawyer yesterday and he wasn't over the shock, even if Weldon Scott had taken the edge off the surprise. Jake now owned controlling share, but the rest had been left to Luke and Zack to split between them. Luke and Zack had agreed to stay for a year, giving Jake a chance to get back on his feet. At the end of the year, he'd buy them out.

Luke wanted to keep his share. He hadn't known how badly until the option was presented to him. He'd always assumed the whole operation would end up Jake's, which was the family tradition—the ranch went to the oldest—but now that he saw the possibilities with the new robotics milking system and biomass power plant, the geek side of him wanted in.

Jake, however, had put in the sweat equity and the long-term business planning. He was the son who'd shared their father's vision. He'd made a significant financial commitment already.

Wanting a piece of his brother's hard work, even though he had no intentions of ever taking it, made Luke uncomfortable. He liked this side of himself even less than the one pursuing Mara. If he had to pick between vices while he was here, he'd go with blue eyes and fiery *vitalidad*. This way, no one got hurt.

Mike gave them a rundown on how to select and enter new games, then left them on their own. The black curtain slid closed and they were alone.

"Lady's choice. Roller coaster first?" Luke inquired. He grabbed the lone chair in the room and dragged it to the round gaming pad on the floor. "You have to sit down for this one."

Her expressive face conveyed her opinion as to what he could do with his chair. "I'm not a child."

No. She certainly was not, and he appreciated that fact.

He pointed to a list of rules on the wall. "'Warning. For your personal safety, gamers are strongly advised to sit down for the roller coaster ride.' It says so, right there." He patted the vinyl cushion. "So sit."

She was far too graceful to do something so mundane. Rather, sliding the headset in place, she settled onto the chair much the same way a ballerina sank into a curtsey at the end of a performance.

Luke watched the screen on the wall as she activated the program. So far, so good.

Less than a minute in, she lifted the headset again. "It's boring sitting down. Let's try something else."

She sounded so disappointed. He couldn't have that. This was supposed to be a fun evening.

"Don't give up yet. I have a solution." He helped her to her feet and got rid of the chair. "Put the headset back on." He stood behind her and wrapped his arms around her waist. The soft mass of her knotted hair brushed the underside of his chin. "Now brace yourself against me. I've got you."

She settled into his arms without an ounce of unease, her butt intimate against his thighs as if they'd been lovers for years. He caught a whiff of mock orange and fought off an urge to explore her throat with his mouth. She smelled delicious. He'd bet she tasted even better.

Meanwhile, her attention was 100 percent immersed in the game. She listed to one side but he steadied her, shifting her upright with his arms and his thighs, and she started to laugh.

"Much better than a chair," she said, wriggling her hips.

He had to agree. The laugh was what got him. Holding her, feeling her weight on his thighs, didn't hurt either.

They played for two hours. She caught on fast, and in fact, when they switched to two-player games, posed a real challenge, because she took the same no-holds-barred approach to competition that he didn't doubt drove her major decisions in life. Impetuosity wasn't usually for him—

he liked to plan—but there was a lot to be said for carpe diem.

He was so glad he'd called her.

It was after eleven when they finally returned to the car. The city was sleeping and the black Montana night sky, glittering thanks to a kaleidoscope of white stars and a bright, crescent moon, stretched forever. It made a man dizzy if he stared up for too long.

What man in his right mind would ever willingly choose to leave here?

Luke choked down the lump of nostalgia. Montana was forever changed for him, now. His home wasn't his anymore. A new generation of McGregors would take over someday— if Jake ever carved out the time to find the right woman. Most women didn't seem interested in ranch life these days.

He saw Mara into the passenger seat, then got behind the wheel. He couldn't remember when he'd last had such a good time. He wasn't ready for the evening to end, but how it ended was up to her.

"I was okay with you cheating at kickboxing," he said as he dug the keys from his pocket, "but pushing me off the ledge on Mount Everest was downright dirty play."

Mara was busy tidying her hair, reinserting the pins that held it in place. He was the one who'd mussed it a little and he couldn't say he was sorry. It looked sexy as hell.

She paused, a pin in one hand, the thick mass of brown hair under the command of the other, and arched an eyebrow. The buttons on the white blouse she wore strained open, allowing him a peek at a frilly pink bra. The color was growing on him.

"I didn't cheat," she insisted, her eyes wide and innocent. "It's hardly my fault that your reflexes are terrible. And dirty how? You were in my way."

"Even so, I believe you promised me a coffee. I'd suggest we go for a drink instead, but I'm driving." Not to mention, Forsyth nightlife wasn't exactly bustling on a Tuesday, so the options for drinks were slim.

She gave her hair one final pat to make sure the knot was secure and lowered her arms. "We passed a little shop on the corner. How about if I treat you to a coffee first, then if you aren't too tired from your fall off that ledge, we can head back to my place for a drink? Or… we could skip the coffee altogether."

He wasn't mistaking her meaning any more than she'd mistaken his. The offer was out there for them both to consider.

But he hadn't been this uncertain about broaching the topic of sex with a woman since he'd been shot down by Susan Adams in high school. Looking back on that, he could see the cards were stacked against him from the start. He'd been a hormone-riddled fourteen-year-old with a penchant for older women, whereas she was a senior who'd only kissed him and let him unfasten her bra because those extra inches he'd grown had made him look old enough for her to forget. He'd been heartbroken for days. A fourteen-year-old boy hadn't understood the difference between lust and love.

He did now. He was most definitely in lust with Mara. He'd been thinking about how good sex with her would be ever since she'd nestled her ass into his crotch earlier on. Possibly before that.

But, while the cards might be more in his favor tonight, he'd just gotten out of a long-term relationship he'd assumed was forever and he wasn't entering another one anytime soon. Mara needed to understand his family came first and the remnants of his career a close second. Women were a far distant third.

The parking lot was empty and so was the street. The only movement was a scrap of paper skittering around the wire garbage can on the curb. The businesses blocking them in on either side of the lot were silent and dark.

"I've really enjoyed tonight," he said. "The past weeks have been rough and I needed a break. But this is a bad time for me to be getting involved with anyone."

"Taking me to a virtual reality room on your night off was a good indicator that you need a break," Mara said, her kind smile understanding. "But no worries, you're in luck. I'm not interested in becoming involved with anyone, either." She placed her palm on his thigh. His blood headed south. Her touch was light, and yet it set off an extraordinary array of sensations. "I've enjoyed tonight, too. Why think it to death? Why can't we just continue to enjoy ourselves without worrying about what happens tomorrow?"

A tight knot deep inside him relaxed. He did think things to death. He'd been doing nothing but thinking for years. He'd been plotting for the better part of two weeks about how to get to know Mara better without becoming too involved, and as it turned out, all he'd had to do was come right out and say it.

As for worrying about tomorrow...

There were a lot of tomorrows between now and next year. Taking them one day at a time definitely seemed the most sensible approach. The only decisions he'd think through without tossing a coin would involve the kids, the ranch, and his brothers.

Carpe diem.

"Coffee is more of a breakfast drink for me," he said, and moved to start the engine.

Mara's fingers curled around his, staying his hand. She edged closer, leaning past the console between them. "There's something we should get out of the way before we begin talking about breakfast."

Of course there was. He was so bad at this.

His gaze zeroed in on her tempting mouth. He'd wanted to taste her all evening—a hard thing to do when they were both wearing headsets—and she'd just given her blessing. He cupped her face in his palms and bent his head over hers, taking a second to appreciate the desire he saw in her amazing eyes. When was the last time a woman had looked at him like this? Or he'd looked at a woman the way he had to be looking at Mara right now?

"I can see you thinking too hard, Dr. Pretty," she whispered.

He swept his thumbs across her cheeks in a light caress. Her eyelashes fluttered. Her skin was so delicate. Smooth.

He covered her mouth with his. She had both hands on his thigh now, bearing her weight. Her fingers curled into his flesh, so close to his crotch that his brain could no longer fully engage, and then, he was no longer thinking at all. He tugged at her bottom lip, tracing it with his tongue. She parted her lips, inviting him in, and he slid his tongue inside her mouth.

His senses exploded from the sight, scent, touch, and taste of her. A small, ragged sigh entered the fray. He couldn't say who it belonged to, but it could well have been his. His hand slid from her cheek to the curve of her throat. Her pulse drummed beneath the pad of his thumb, making him so hard it ached.

His brain gave an insistent rap on his skull, calling on the one sense he'd yet to engage. What the hell was going on, here?

What was he doing?

They broke apart. Mara's eyes were wide and startled, her breathing as unsteady as his. He had no words for what had just happened between them, but whatever it was, if he had to guess, he'd say she'd felt it, too.

And it wasn't what either of them had expected. Breakfast, at least for tomorrow, was out of the question.

"It's late," he said. "I'll take you home."

Chapter Five

T HEY BEGAN THE drive home. Traffic on the highway was light. Stars twinkled in the night sky above.

And Dr. Pretty looked so completely freaked out that Mara didn't know whether she should feel insulted or laugh.

She tucked her hands under her thighs. They were shaking a little. She hadn't expected the chemistry to be quite so high either, but she wasn't about to allow the evening to end in awkwardness and emotional withdrawal because of a physical—and very mutual—attraction.

Luke had needed tonight. He'd needed fun. Sex, however, would only complicate things for him. And she did not need the angst those complications would cause. She'd finally pulled her own life back together and she planned to keep it that way.

This was her cue to run.

"We've started off on the wrong foot," Mara said. "Neither one of us is interested in a relationship, so maybe we're moving too fast in the wrong direction. We both had a great time tonight. Why don't we try being friends, instead?"

Relief dragged him a few steps back from the edge. "It's not you, it's me."

"Oh, don't worry. It's definitely you," she assured him, smiling to take the bluntness from her words. "I was more than willing to cook you breakfast, but I don't think you're ready for that."

His intense, black-lashed green eyes delved deep into hers. "My family life is a mess and I need to help sort it out. My sister's kids need stability and a real home, and they've only got three uncles who have no clue what they're doing to provide it."

"*Run,*" her head whispered.

But she loved kids, too. She worked with them every day. She also understood the commitment caring for them involved, and the caregiver's need for adult interaction. "I really do understand. Grand isn't exactly the place to get away from it all, is it?"

That earned her a smile as he unwound a bit more. A muscle flexed in his cheek, indicating the ghost of a smile.

"Everyone here is pretty much up in your business," he conceded.

"So I've noticed." Her broken lock came to mind, but she didn't point out that he'd been up in hers, too.

They rolled along for a few miles. Then…

"Why do you call me Dr. Pretty?" he asked.

She rubbed the heel of her hand along the length of the console. She had to quit thinking of him that way because it kept slipping out. His name was Luke. "Nobody's ever told you how attractive you are?"

"Maybe when I was six. These days, most people tend admire me more for my mind."

By most people she assumed he meant women, and yet, no matter how smart he was, she found it hard to believe that any sexually aware woman could discount his physical appearance, too.

"Dr. Pretty covers both beauty and brains," she said.

An eyebrow lifted. His hard, Greek-statue profile unbent. The side-eye he cast her voiced his opinion better than words, although he gave it a shot. "My ego thanks you. I think."

Mara straightened her legs. They were back where they'd been an hour ago—on comfortable ground. Any more talk and things might get weird again, so she kept her peace, and instead, put some thought into that kiss and getting her own head in order.

She'd been kissed lots of times in her life and was far from a prude. Traveling so much, especially when she was in her teens, meant she'd had her heart broken more than once, too, although she'd left that kind of emotional drama behind when she became an adult. Little Zee had caused little more than a dent in her pride and her finances. Things could have been worse. What bothered her most was that she'd fallen for his pitiful story.

Luke's story was real. He'd lost a large part of his family. He had an orphaned niece and two nephews to help transition to Grand, and was obviously struggling with it.

Maybe she should focus more on his needs and less on hers, because they'd had very different reactions to the kiss they'd just shared. She'd been willing to straddle him and take him right there. He'd looked ready to cut and run.

"Tell me about your dance studio," he said. "Do you like teaching?"

"I love it." But did she love it better than dancing?

Only time could confirm or deny that. She didn't yet earn a living wage from teaching, whereas before her accident, she'd been one of the more successful dancers in an industry notorious for its low-income wages. A tiny knife twisted. She chose to ignore it.

"I wish I had more male students, though," she added, throwing it out there to see what he'd say. Most of the cowboys she'd met, while thrilled to sign their daughters up for lessons, seemed to view their young sons taking formal dance training as a direct attack on their manhood. They didn't care that two of the greatest ballet dancers of all time—Vasiliev and Baryshnikov—were straight.

She'd met Baryshnikov once. Even though he was now in his seventies, he still made her swoon. A man who knew how to move…

That was so, so sexy.

"If getting boys on board is your goal, you should try coaching football or hockey," Luke said. "There's more money in sports. Most fathers bet on their sons making the NFL or NHL, not the national ballet."

This wasn't news. "Dance is as much a sport as it is an art."

"I agree, but I'm explaining how the Grand hive mind works. If there's no potential for money, then they aren't going to pay for lessons. Dancing is for dreamers."

She could have told him she'd been a high earner, but

saw no point in it, because she wasn't a success anymore. In fact, she was spending a lot more than she made. She'd never made as much money as a professional football player, either. Not even dancing for Little Zee.

Besides, she had the feeling she was missing something important. He sounded jaded, and not as if he agreed with the "hive mind," as he called it, at all. She wondered if he'd been considered a dreamer, growing up.

"Not every football player is going to turn pro," she said. "Neither is every dancer. Those are high expectations. Besides, money isn't everything. Sometimes it's simply about participating in an activity you love."

"You can't live on love."

"No, but you can love to live. Dancing is about expressing your feelings. You should try it sometime."

His eyebrows pinched in surprise. He looked at her as they pulled up to the flashing red Marion Street lights. "You think I don't know how to dance?"

Poor, oblivious Dr. Pretty. That wasn't the skill she called into question. He couldn't help but be a decent dancer. He moved with too much style to be anything else.

But he had to quit thinking so much.

"I bet you and your avatar do a fantastic one-step," she said.

He chuckled a little. "We do okay." He rolled through the flashing lights, checking for oncoming traffic, before speaking again. "My sister Liz studied dance in New York, but gave it up when she and Blair got married. I don't think she ever had any plans to dance professionally. She just wanted to go to New York. Our dad complained all the time about how much money her dreams cost him, and yet, in the end, it was his dream that killed them."

Mara's heart whipped out a fouetté. It hurt for him. "I'm so sorry."

"Don't be. I'm not advocating for people to give up on their dreams."

He'd lost her. Again. "Then what are you advocating?"

"Nothing, really. Just thinking out loud."

The car hit a bump in the road as they made the turn onto her street. A few minutes later, she was home.

Luke's gaze drifted, just for a second, to the cemetery gate. The muscle under his right eye flinched, then his cheek smoothed. He turned the car off. The motor made faint clicking noises as it shut down.

He helped her from the car, then walked her to the door. They both stood there for a moment, things awkward again. Moths flittered around the light mounted over the door. She slid her key in the lock and jiggled the knob until the lock gave. She debated asking him again if he'd like to come in, just for a coffee, and decided against it.

Too much baggage. He's in a bad place.

"Thank you," she said, her hand on the knob. "I had a great time, tonight."

"I did, too. Maybe we can try it again."

"I'd like that."

He pressed his lips to her cheek. "I'll call you."

She wondered how many weeks it might take him this time, or if he really would call.

He was gone before she had the door fully open.

She closed the door behind her and leaned her back against it, scrunching her eyelids together and touching her fingertips to her cheek. Her *abuela* kissed with more heat. Her fingers trailed to her lips.

So, however, did Luke—when he didn't put quite so much thought into it.

LUKE STOOD NEXT to the computer screen in one of the new barn's four robotic milking rooms and watched through the thick pane of glass as the robot arm latched the cups onto the cows that passed through the gate. A ration of grain helped lure them in. The cow's ear tag was read at the gate by an automatic identification system. The system recorded information about the animal—how much milk it gave, and how much grain it consumed, for starters. If she was due to be milked, the gate opened.

Lately, one of the sensors on this robot had been malfunctioning. Luke thought he had it fixed, but hung around to make sure.

Besides, he was in no hurry to head back to the house. He'd had a disagreement with Jake at breakfast over Finn.

He should have known not to bring up a sensitive subject when Jake was in a bad mood. It turned out his brother still had a thing for Lacey Anderson, the girl he'd dated in high school. And Lacey, as luck would have it, was a teacher at the Marion Street elementary school, which the boys now attended.

Luke wasn't sure what had happened between Jake and Lacey last night—as far as he knew, Jake had gone to a parent-teacher meeting—but one thing was guaranteed. Jake's evening hadn't ended any better than Luke's.

Luke did know what had gone wrong with Mara. It was his fault for the way their date had ended. He had no idea why he'd been such an ass about her dance classes, other than that he hated to see her get her hopes up about attracting male students. If Jake's reaction to Luke's suggestion they put Finn in dance was any indication, she'd get them up for nothing.

But when she'd talked about male students, and she'd sounded so wistful, he'd thought of Finn. Liz had signed him up for a summer dance class in New York. He'd seen it noted in her calendar when they'd packed up the kids and their belongings. He'd barely paid attention to it then because they'd all had so much on their minds, but now that Mara had reminded him of it, he saw no reason not to carry through with his sister's plans.

Unfortunately Jake—the kids' legal guardian—wasn't on board. His objection was that Finn was already having a hard enough time fitting in at school, and putting him in dance wouldn't help.

Luke adjusted the sleeves of his barn coverall. He'd gone along with every other childrearing decision to date, but he was their uncle too, and he should get a say. To hell with his older brother. When he hadn't fit in, Jake was the one who'd taught him to lead with his left. Finn was taking those dance lessons even if Jake had to teach him to fight, too.

This had nothing to do with wanting to see Mara again so he could make it up to her for how last night had ended.

The cow finished her grain, the cups disengaged, and the gate swung open, setting her free. Luke checked the cow's data on the screen on the computer. Everything was in order. The sensor appeared to be functioning.

With the barn chores attended to, he had work to catch up on for the college. They'd given him six months. After that, he had nothing. He stepped out of the barn, turning his thoughts in another direction. The sun burned hot in the cloudless sky. The dry spell seemed in no danger of ending anytime soon.

The ranch house faced the Tongue River, which cut through part of the McGregor land. One of their enterprising ancestors had begun an irrigation system that functioned well to this day, so the cattle were in no danger of dying of thirst. The same couldn't be said for the grass. They'd have to make hay soon and try to get it in while the quality was high.

He entered the house through the mudroom behind the kitchen, kicked off his rubber barn boots, and hung his coverall next to the door. He washed his hands in the laundry tub. When he entered the bright kitchen, Zack was on the floor next to the oak table, playing with Lydia.

"Hey," Luke said. "Where were you two all morning?"

Zack shrugged, a mean trick to pull off while on his hands and knees, growling at Lydia, pretending to nip at her belly. Lydia squealed and shoved at his face with her pudgy baby hands. She had the cutest hair ever, all fluffy and blond like the down on a newly-hatched chick. Drool spilled from her plump lower lip to her chin.

"Where were you last night?" Zack shot back.

Luke didn't answer, and while neither had Zack, Luke was positive his brother had been visiting the neighbor again.

Posey Davies had a daughter a little older than Lydia and no husband that Luke could discern. Posey seemed nice enough, although very reserved. She had a lost waif image going on, what with her white-blond hair and big eyes. He suspected there was a lot more to her story, and worried about Zack, who had a weakness for helpless women, becoming caught up in it. Where there was a baby, there was usually a baby's father.

He scooped Lydia off the floor, rescuing her from whatever wild animal Zack was pretending to be. At least Liz and Blair could rest easy knowing that at least one of their children was settling into ranch life without any trouble.

"Liz signed Finn up for dance lessons this summer," he said. "Grand has a teacher, but when I mentioned it to Jake, he was dead set against it. What would you think if I put Finn in dance lessons behind his back?"

Zack rocked onto his heels. His socks were striped navy and gray. His T-shirt and jeans were both navy. Dark red hair stood up in clumps thanks to Lyddie tangling her fingers in it. He looked eighteen, not twenty-eight.

"I'd think what Jake doesn't know won't hurt him. He can't keep track of everything that happens around here. That's why he asked us to help out. And," he added, a smirk on his face, "I think the dance teacher is hot."

Luke played it cool. "So I've heard."

"C'mon," Zack complained. He got to his feet. "So things didn't work out with Denise. Get back in the saddle."

Luke kept his focus on Lydia. He held her above his head and blew on her belly where her yellow jersey had hiked up. A cute pair of blue shorts—likely inherited from one of her brothers—covered her diaper-padded round butt. "Eventually. Not yet."

Zack changed the subject. "Are you really okay with staying in Grand for a year?"

They hadn't had much of a chance to talk about the will in the two days since the Wagging Tongue's lawyer had dropped the bombshell on them.

"I am." Luke lowered Lydia into his arms. She patted his cheeks. Man, she was cute. "I'm not okay with taking a quarter of something that's rightfully Jake's."

"Jake doesn't see it that way."

"I know he doesn't." Lydia grew tired of being held, so Luke set her down. She toddled over to the toy box in the corner and began tossing the contents on the floor. Luke looked his brother in the eye. "How do you see it?"

"I think the ranch is growing. With the right planning it could support two families. Possibly three," Zack added, a little too hastily, and the light bulb came on.

"You want to keep your share?" Luke asked, to be sure.

"I'm thinking about it."

A glimmer of hope he hadn't known he possessed disappeared. Zack was an accountant. He was also excellent with animals and kids. If Jake wanted a partner, then Zack was the likeliest choice, because he brought added value.

He'd also said "families," not people.

Luke forgot his disappointment, exchanging it for concern. "Does this decision to stay have something to do with Posey?"

"Please. She won't give me the time of day. I've missed Grand, that's all."

But Zack's gaze no longer held his, and Luke's unease expanded. If she wouldn't give him the time of day it was because he'd expressed interest, and Luke knew his brother. He wasn't the kind of man to back down once he started after something he wanted. If Posey wasn't interested in him, that was one thing. Zack would come to his senses. If she was holding back for some other reason, however—maybe one that involved her baby's MIA father—then the McGregors might have a problem.

Luke was tired of problems. They had enough without factoring in women. Jake was in a foul mood over Lacey. Zack had issues with Posey. Meanwhile, Luke?

If he had a problem, it was of his own making. Mara was worry-free. She was fun and made no demands. Last night could have ended on a far different note if he hadn't been so unprepared for that kiss. The next time he took her out, he'd know what to expect and be better prepared.

First, he'd sign Finn up for that class.

"Grand does have something special about it," he agreed.

Chapter Six

"**I** DON'T WANNA dance," Finn announced. "Dance is for girls."

It was Saturday morning. Jake had taken Mac to soccer practice and Zack was baking cookies with Lydia. Zack would cover for Luke if Jake got home first. It wasn't that they planned on lying to Jake, or that it really mattered whether or not he found out. Jake genuinely wanted what was best for the kids. They'd agreed this was a need-to-know situation and they had it under control.

Luke glanced in the rearview mirror. His nephew slouched as far as he could in his seat. He had his arms crossed, lower lip thrust out, and wore a dark scowl on his face. He looked so much like Zack when he didn't get his own way that Luke wanted to laugh. The only difference was that Finn had the green McGregor eyes while Zack's eyes were blue.

Luke hadn't anticipated resistance from Finn. He'd assumed Liz had signed him up for dance because he'd expressed an interest. Now he was beginning to suspect that the interest was all on Liz's part and she'd hoped Finn might pick it up.

"What makes you think it's for girls?" he asked Finn.

"Daddy says so. He says Mommy can put Lyddie in dance when she's older."

Luke didn't miss the use of present tense. Finn, in his five-year-old head, had a problem understanding that his parents weren't coming back. Jake was considering getting both boys into therapy, and while Luke wholeheartedly agreed, he also believed that, in Finn's case, time would take care of it. He simply wasn't old enough yet to have a frame of reference for death.

And as for Blair's opinion about dance… Luke would have loved to be a fly on the wall for that conversation. Liz hadn't been a militant feminist, but she'd been all about equal rights.

"Dance isn't only for girls," he assured Finn. "Who do you think lifts them when they do those fancy moves?"

Finn chewed on that. The scowl eased into a frown. "Bigger girls?"

"Possibly," Luke said. "Personally though, I like dancing with girls. Maybe they'd like to dance with boys sometimes, too."

"Why?"

"Why not? What's wrong with girls and boys dancing?"

Luke waited.

"You dance with girls?" Finn finally asked, suspicion rife in his tone.

"I do," Luke replied. He took another quick peek in the mirror. Finn looked a lot less sure of his stance. "Do you really not want to dance?" he asked. Because if he didn't,

Luke would turn the car around now. He didn't need an excuse to see Mara again. He'd wanted to please her, yes, but not at Finn's expense.

It took Finn a second to answer. "I don't want to lift girls."

"I don't think that's anything you need to worry about your first day," Luke replied. "The boys who lift girls have had a lot of lessons. You don't have to dance with girls if you don't want to, either. But why don't you give lessons a try before you make up your mind?"

"Fine. I'll try one. But that's it."

By the time they reached Mara's, the small parking lot in front of the cemetery was full and Luke had to park on the street. He unfastened Finn from his seat and held his hand as they walked to the studio door. While the street was a dead end and hardly busy Finn had the attention span of a squirrel and zero concept of danger. None of the McGregors trusted his common sense. The rule was, especially on the ranch where large machines were in constant motion, that if there was a vehicle around, an adult had to hang on to him.

The door to the studio was open, so Luke and Finn walked in. About ten little girls were running around the large space like leotard-clad chickens on crack, jumping on the mats and hanging off the barres. The mirrored walls multiplied their numbers tenfold.

Finn, for his part, forgot all about his aversion to girls. He shook off Luke's hand and tore across the room to join the melee. The girls greeted him with equal enthusiasm, proving there was no explaining what went on in kids' heads.

Luke had no idea how Mara planned to tame this mad-house. All he could say was good luck.

A gaggle of what he assumed to be mothers were crowd-ed around a small table near the stairs where Mara was taking registration. Her head was bent and she hadn't yet seen him. A few of the women noted his presence, however, and the chatter gradually died down.

The sudden attention had nothing to do with him being the lone male in their midst. He'd rather it did. He and his brothers had been a hot topic of gossip for weeks and it seemed the interest in their family situation hadn't yet tapered off.

Mara finally lifted her head to see why the mothers around her had gone quiet. Blue eyes met his. Thick dark lashes fluttered as if she couldn't quite believe what she saw. Then her gaze trailed to the passel of unholy terrors. She zeroed in on the redheaded newcomer at once. Her eyes, widening, flew back to Luke's face and he had the uneasy impression that she thought he was humoring her by bring-ing his nephew for lessons.

That wasn't what he'd intended at all.

She would never challenge him in front of an audience, however. Instead, she smiled at him as if they'd never met. He had a flashback to the other night in his car. She'd worn a far different smile then, until he'd gone and ruined it.

No more of that.

"Welcome," she said, and held up a sheet of paper. "Can I ask you to fill out one of these forms?"

Making his way through the silent group of women

couldn't have been any more uncomfortable if he'd been stark naked. He'd gone to school with a few of them, although most were closer to Jake's age than his. Their slight, not-quite-hidden smiles said they knew exactly why he was here.

He nodded to everyone, acknowledging them the way he would a group of freshmen, then he concentrated on Mara and tried to ignore everything else. She wore a black leotard and tights, a filmy pink wrap-around skirt, and well-worn ballet slippers that might once have been white. She'd wound her mass of dark hair into a tight, ballerina-style bun. She looked elegant, professional, and of course, stunning. She lit up the space around her, casting the other women in shadow.

When she rose to pass him the form and a pen, however, he noticed the bandage wrapped thigh-to-calf under her tights, and the way her knee didn't quite bend when she resumed her seat.

"I didn't get a chance to pick up proper dance clothes for Finn," Luke said, clutching the form. He'd dressed him in a pair of gray sweatpants and a Spider-Man T-shirt. "If you tell me what to buy I'll make sure he has it for next week."

Mara dug another sheet of paper out of her pile. "Here you go. This has all the information you need."

"She offers Zumba classes on Wednesdays and Thursdays for adults," one of the mothers added, her eyes twinkling. "If you'd like a class for yourself, too."

"Thanks," Luke said. "I'll keep that in mind. I've put on a little weight thanks to the desk job and my thighs could do with some toning."

The women all laughed. He withdrew to one of the chairs near the door while he could. He filled out the form and returned it to Mara. He noticed the mothers were leaving.

"Mind if I hang around?" he asked.

"Actually," Mara said, "I'd prefer it if you came back in an hour. The children need to learn to pay attention to me, not their parents." Her cheeks dimpled. "Or their uncles."

Luke wasn't sure that leaving Finn here without him was such a good idea. The boy could be a handful. The little girls weren't much better, however, not from what he could see, and Mara seemed unperturbed, so he didn't argue. He'd sit in the car for an hour and keep an eye on the door in case Finn escaped.

When he walked outside, the mothers pounced on him like lions on prey.

"We usually head down to the Wayside Café for coffee while we wait," one woman said. "Would you like to join us?"

Luke was about to come up with an excuse to say no. Spending an hour with a group of women talking about their husbands and kids didn't appeal to him in the least. Plus, Grand women were nosy. His mother had been one, so he had firsthand experience. He could see this turning into a really uncomfortable situation where he was asked a lot of questions about his nephews and niece, his brothers, and their plans for the future, and he'd have no answers.

But before he could find one, however, he remembered

he'd just left Finn with ten little girls because he'd asked him to give it a chance before he made up his mind.

"I'd love to join you," he said.

The morning was hot and sunny. Again. Not a cloud in the sky. The short walk to the Wayside Café took them down the cul-de-sac to Yellowstone Drive, which meandered the river front—hence the name—and through Grand's business district.

Luke discovered that a lot had changed since high school. One of the mothers was a lawyer who ran her own practice. One was a doctor, and another, a marketing executive. Only one of them was a ranch wife.

"We're a dying breed," she said cheerfully.

Luke understood why. His mother had raised a family, did the ranch bookkeeping, and helped out in the milking parlor her entire married life. She'd raised more fur babies than children. She'd also been deeply involved in the community, immersing herself in fund-raising and social programs. He'd never thought twice about everything she did when he was a kid. Now, he could see how much of her life she'd devoted to family, community, and ranching. Had she ever wanted more for herself? Or something different?

Regret pricked his heart. He'd never know.

The group squeezed onto the Wayside Café's patio, which jutted over the river, and pulled several wooden tables together in the center. Wrought iron bistro tables lined the railings. Fishermen drifted lazily by in their boats. Luke had spent many hours studying here when he was in high school.

He wrestled an enormous blue-and-yellow striped sun

umbrella open to offer the women some shade. Everyone took turns placing their orders inside at the counter before settling in.

Then, Luke waited for the inquisition to start, wondering if it would begin with the children, his brothers, or Mara.

"If Finn's any indication, the children seem to be settling in well," one woman remarked. Her name was Pam. She was the marketing executive.

"So far, so good," Luke agreed, even though really, both boys were having some issues. All of Grand didn't need to weigh in on them.

"If Jake wants to get them into counseling, have him call me. I know an excellent child psychologist," Felicity said. She was the doctor, and she and Liz had been friends. Luke remembered her coming to the house when she was a teenager. Kind eyes and a warm presence about her reassured whoever she focused on that everything was going to be fine.

"Lacey Anderson has already given him a few names," he replied, throwing his brother under the bus.

"That explains why Jake has Mac signed up for soccer," the lawyer said. Luke couldn't remember her name. "They dated back in high school, didn't they? Are they an item again?"

"I couldn't say."

He regretted bringing up Lacey's name. Jake had taken it hard when she broke up with him back when they were teenagers, and Luke would like to see them work things out now that they were adults. He had no wish to jinx it. Jake deserved to find happiness. Luke's real goal had been to deflect their attention from him.

The lawyer was nodding as if in complete understanding. "So Jake takes Mac to soccer, which his former girlfriend coaches, and you take Finn to dance, which is run by a woman so hot, if I wasn't already married, I'd consider turning for her. I see a developing pattern. The boys have a baby sister too, don't they? And don't you have another brother who's single? Who's running the Grand preschool?" She directed the last question to the table in general, and everyone laughed, Luke included.

"Wow, women are mean," he complained, not minding at all that their fun was at his expense. He much preferred their teasing to the usual awkward stretches of silence that nobody knew how to fill whenever his family was mentioned. "Finn's mom was a dancer. Wasn't she, Felicity?"

Felicity took a long sip of her latte and side-eyed him with raised eyebrows before confirming his claim. "She was. But I don't see what that's got to do with how hot Mara is."

If he tried to deny that he found Mara hot, he'd be chum in the water. No one would believe him. So how should he play this?

"You've caught me," he said. "I put Finn in dance so I'd have an excuse to get close. You all seem to know her. How should I go about asking her out?"

More laughter followed.

"We're just messing with you," the ranch wife—Cossette—assured him. "Mara is a wonderful person, but she doesn't seem to be interested in the local men. She needed to get away from all the attention after her break up with Little

Zee and nobody in Grand would talk to the press."

She'd been more than a dancer for Little Zee, huh?

He hadn't picked up on that, although he probably should have. She didn't talk about her dance career, only her studio, and she'd assured him she wasn't interested in becoming involved with anyone either. He was bad at putting the pieces together. He wondered what had gone wrong between her and the pop star. She had to be the one who'd bowed out. He couldn't imagine any man being so stupid as to pass up on a woman like Mara.

Present company excepted.

"So she doesn't date?" he asked, curious to find out more about her taste in men and where he might fit in. He hadn't imagined the heat in their kiss.

"Not seriously," Cossette said. "Cowboys are a novelty to her. She hasn't gone out with the same man more than once. Plus, Grand is pretty quiet for someone who's used to the kind of life a pop star leads. Now that paparazzi interest in her relationship with Little Zee has died down, she won't be staying."

The other women concurred.

Rather than dissuade him, however, he was further intrigued. He recalled Mara's words the other night in his car. *"Why think it to death? Why can't we just continue to enjoy ourselves without worrying about what happens tomorrow?"*

"I'm not a cowboy," he said. And he and Mara weren't dating—not in the traditional Grand sense. He got why she'd be reluctant to go out with the same man more than once, though. In Grand, that made a woman as good as engaged.

"Of course you are." Felicity sounded surprised there would be any doubt. "The McGregors founded Grand. Your family has ranched here since the mid-eighteen hundreds. Once a Montanan, always a Montanan. A PhD isn't going to change that."

It was her surprise—mirrored on the other faces around the table—that finally made him feel as if he'd returned to a place where he had a chance to belong. He'd never had a sense of being in the right place in Seattle, where his life was all about his career. He'd never had it in Grand before, either.

But whose fault was that?

These women hadn't allowed their careers to change who they were. They were proud of their roots. When had he begun burying his?

"Besides," Felicity continued, donning a thoughtful expression, "I don't believe that Mara isn't interested in cowboys. The problem is that cowboys see her as a challenge and approach her the same way they would an unbroken prize horse. She's not ready to be roped into settling down, and even if she were, it's unlikely a ranch life would suit her. This isn't her world."

Luke took a hit of his coffee and pictured Mara jumping off the ledge of the Empire State Building at Reality Bytes. When her dance career ended, she hadn't sat around and complained, either—she'd shifted goals.

The women might have a good handle on cowboys, and on him, too, but he didn't believe they'd read Mara right.

Not at all.

The sun beat on his unprotected back, heating his skin through his cotton shirt. A young couple in their teens wandered through the glass door onto the patio. They beelined for one of the bistro tables overlooking the Yellowstone River, where they proceeded to hold hands and ignore the view in favor of staring into each other's eyes.

He felt a little sorry for them. They'd never survive the real world. Fortunately, he was well past that kind of angst-riddled puppy love. He was looking forward to his next nondate with Mara, where the expectations were set.

She owed him a coffee.

"Poor Finn," Luke said, taking another sip of his coffee. "I dragged him to dance lessons for nothing."

"HEELS TOGETHER," MARA said, reminding the children of first position while they finished their lesson at the barre.

They were a wonderful group of girls.

As for Finn…

She took a few minutes to help him straighten his form, pressing one hand under his ribs and the other at the base of his spine, showing him again how to bend his knees with his heels pressed together while he held on to the barre.

At first she'd assumed Luke had brought him to class to prove some sort of point and she'd been annoyed. She couldn't figure out Luke's thought processes at all. But twenty minutes into the class, it had become clear that Finn had his uncle's innate flair for movement, combined with a complete lack of inhibition, and she'd become excited instead. It no longer mattered what Luke's motives might be. Finn was a natural.

Plus, he was a charmer. It was cute the way the girls in the class all did their best to maneuver into position beside him and he took it in stride. His attention span could use a little work, although that would come with age. A lot of his restlessness no doubt had to do with the death of his parents and the subsequent move to Grand, the poor little guy. Dance might help him express his feelings in a healthy way.

And those big green eyes of his... Beneath the fringe of red lashes, they were the exact same shade as his uncle's.

So, by the time Luke returned to retrieve his nephew, Mara was no longer annoyed. She had a talented new male student who was a pleasure to teach, which was all that mattered.

The mothers collected their daughters.

Finn leaped into his uncle's arms, a move that didn't faze Luke in the slightest. He pretended to stagger under the child's weight, which could be no more than forty-five pounds soaking wet.

"Whoa, bud. How much muscle did you pack on in one lesson?"

Finn held Luke's cheeks in his small palms and stared into his eyes, their noses a hair's breadth apart. Mara had to bite the inside of her lip to keep from laughing. It was a classic child move to capture an adult's undivided attention.

"I want to come back for another lesson tomorrow," the

boy demanded, leaving no room for doubt as to how serious he was.

"Miss Ramos doesn't offer this class on Sundays," Luke replied. "Besides, I need to get you the right clothes to wear first. How about if I bring you back next Saturday, instead?" He shot Mara an unspoken query, his eyebrows uplifted, and Mara's breath snagged in her lungs. "That's assuming Miss Ramos wants you."

"I do," she said.

She wanted his uncle even more. She couldn't explain why. Montana was full of beautiful men. So was the world. And yet it was this one, with his layers of complexity, who couldn't seem to stop his brain from spinning in multiple directions, who fascinated her the most.

With his nephew perched on his hip, and the pair looking so natural together, he pulled his phone from his pocket. He flicked his thumbs over the screen. Seconds later her phone, on the small table she'd used to register students, pinged that a text had come in.

She picked it up and took a quick, casual glance at the message.

"Tonight?"

She didn't dare look in his direction. She tapped the screen on her phone and sent him an equally spare response that consisted of the number *8*. Then, her heart pounding so hard she couldn't believe the whole room didn't hear it, she set her phone down.

No one had paid any attention, at least, not that she could tell. The mothers were listening to their daughters' chatter. Luke had Finn by the hand and they were already halfway out the door.

"Wave goodbye to Miss Ramos," Luke said, and Finn pumped his arm in a wide arc over his head. A broad smile exposed the gap in his gums where a baby tooth had come out. He was as hard to resist as his uncle.

She got another text a few minutes later.

"I like my coffee with bacon and eggs."

Chapter Seven

MARA EXAMINED HER living space with a critical eye, making sure everything was in place.

The apartment was as long as the warehouse downstairs, although only a third as wide. The door from the catwalk opened into her kitchen. She'd dipped into her savings to make this a home. She'd bought high-end, stainless-steel and ceramic appliances because she liked to cook to unwind while she listened to music. She didn't own a television. She'd invested in a sound system, instead.

She'd replaced the chipped laminate island countertop with granite and bought four barstools at her own expense. A dinette set for two nestled under one of the windows, giving her the view of the river she loved. Its waters sparkled with light after dark. The laundry room and bathroom shared space off the kitchen.

Her living room occupied the center of the wide open space. It contained a cream-colored lounge chair, dozens of throw cushions, and a sleek, orange-leather, L-shaped sofa that divided it from her bed and the tall wooden wardrobe at the far end of the room. A love seat that matched the sofa faced the window. She'd bought a folding screen to section off one corner of her bedroom space and turned it into a dressing area so she could toss her clothes around and leave her makeup out without having to look at the mess.

Because the loft apartment had once been broken into offices, three large windows provided a great deal of light and a spectacular view. She'd bought blinds that blocked the heat of the sun but allowed her to see out without anyone outside seeing in. Three overhead fluorescent lights each operated off separate switches where doors leading to the catwalk had been. She'd shut off all but the one in the kitchen, and she'd set the dimmer to low.

This was her first real home and she loved it. Always, before, she'd done so much traveling that in terms of personal space, hotel rooms had held as much meaning for her. But she'd come to Grand needing a place to withdraw from the world and recover, like an animal licking its wounds, and she was protective of the haven she'd made for herself. Other than Diana, and her friend Lacey, she didn't entertain people here.

Luke would be the first man she allowed in.

A bottle of sparkling wine chilled in an ice bucket on the dinette table, along with two crystal flutes. A tray of canapés she'd made that afternoon was stored in the fridge. Soft music strained from the wall-mounted speakers.

Too intimate? Too obvious?

What did it matter? They both knew where the evening was headed. The trick would be in keeping Dr. Pretty from thinking too much about it.

She'd chosen a smock-style, flowered sleeveless top that

flowed to mid-thigh over cropped white leggings and flip-flops. She wore her hair down, and other than a pink-tinted lip balm and a hint of eyeliner, hadn't bothered with makeup. Luke hadn't given her any hints as to what to wear, only that he planned to be here for breakfast, so she assumed they'd be staying in the entire night.

The doorbell rang at eight o'clock sharp. She took her time descending the stairs, afraid if she rushed, her leg would give out and she'd roll to the bottom. She'd never hear the end of it if she did.

When she opened the door, Luke greeted her with a bouquet of orange tiger lilies in one hand. He had on a white cotton shirt, hipster jeans, white canvas shoes without socks, and… a tan-colored Stetson. Computer-Geek-Gone-Cowboy was her first astonished impression.

Or maybe she had that backward.

Either way, the look worked for him. The black-framed glasses tucked into the breast pocket of his shirt were a nice added touch. She was sure there was some sort of symbolism going on, but she had no idea what it was, or its purpose.

She did know she found the combination oddly appealing, although she would never have guessed that a geeky cowboy was even close to a turn-on, no matter how gorgeous he was.

He leaned in and kissed her. "You look beautiful," he said, handing her the bouquet, and she laughed, because he sounded so pleased about getting his opening line right.

She clutched the flowers to her chest. "Thank you. I didn't know you wore glasses."

Confusion etched his face. He touched the bridge of his nose, patted his pocket, and then, the confusion cleared.

"I forgot about them," he confessed. "I wear them when I'm on the computer. I was grading papers, trying to get ahead on some work while Jake and Zack got the kids ready for bed."

She had to ask. "And the hat?"

He grinned at her, showing a flash of straight white teeth. Green eyes crinkled. For the first time since she met him, he looked truly carefree and she got a glimpse of the man he might really be. He ran his thumb along the brim of his hat. "I thought I'd dress up for the occasion."

He reclaimed the flowers and carried them upstairs, sticking close behind her. His protectiveness had annoyed her at first. She found macho displays oppressive. But Luke displayed no signs of possessiveness, only good manners, and those, she chose to enjoy. She didn't mind being treated with respect—she disliked a man thinking he owned her.

Luke returned the flowers to her at the top of the stairs. She led him through the open door of her apartment and got a great deal of satisfaction out of the look on his face as he took it all in. Twilight had barely begun to settle, and with the blinds open and the kitchen light on, every nook was exposed. Music from *La Boheme* drifted in the air. She'd danced the part of Mimi in Germany one summer ten years ago while she was a student. The music made her both happy and sad.

She found a vase for the flowers and put them in water.

"This apartment looks nothing like what I'd expect based

on the outside," Luke said.

He'd removed his hat. She relieved him of it and carried it through the living space to the bedroom area, setting it on the foot of her bed, then returned to the kitchen, where he'd pulled up a barstool at the island. He was watching her in a way that made her pulse race. He'd kicked off his shoes and was in his bare feet, one on the floor, the other propped on a rung of the stool.

"You dance when you walk," he observed.

"So do you." She blurted it out without thinking.

The corners of his lips crooked upward. "Do I?"

He thought she was teasing him.

"You do," she insisted, and there, in the middle of the living room, she mimicked his movements. "You move like this."

"That's amazing." His tone shifted to admiration. "That you can imitate someone so well, I mean," he added for clarification, "although I don't make walking look quite so... sexual."

"Yes, you do. It was the first thing I noticed about you. I thought you might be a dancer." He'd definitely made her think about sex. It was all she could think about now. It was going to be good, if the kiss they'd shared in his car was any indication.

It was also why he was here.

"I'm flattered," he said. He continued to watch her. "What else did you notice about me?"

She remembered he rarely received compliments that didn't reflect his intelligence. Had no woman truly ever told him how beautiful he was?

She found that so sad. True beauty was about more than physical appearance, however. That was only another part of the package. Presentation mattered, too. So what compliment could she pay him that showed she'd been paying attention to everything about him?

Because it was the complete package that fascinated her so. She couldn't wait to unwrap him.

His eyes said she didn't have to.

She wriggled between his knees and draped her arms over his shoulders. His thighs tightened around her legs, anchoring her to him, and his hands cupped her hips. Her mouth hovered above his, their lips not quite touching. He'd shaved. She caught the soft, clean scent of sandalwood.

"Your eyes," she said. They were such a unique shade of green. "You were so very intent on your mission. How did the focaccia turn out, by the way?"

"It was delicious." His voice had turned husky. He tracked the tip of his tongue along the outer ridge of her bottom lip. "So are you."

She tugged on the tails of his shirt, freeing them from his jeans, slid her hands underneath to the flat plane of his belly, and lowered her mouth. She hadn't intended for things to progress quite this fast, but she wasn't going to give him a chance to do any thinking. He'd been so good with Finn today—patient and funny—and that was the man she wanted here in her haven, and inside her, tonight.

Luke's hands stayed on her hips, steadying her, as she kissed him. His fingers tightened. And then, he lifted her so she was straddling his thighs. She unbuttoned his shirt. They broke apart long enough for her to push it from his shoulders and him to peel her blouse off over her head. The garments dropped to the floor, leaving him in his jeans and her in a pink demi-cup and leggings. He scrabbled around for something in his pocket, then tossed a handful of condoms onto the island.

"Are you okay with this?" he asked, searching her face.

She took his face in her hands the way Finn had that morning. "Of course I'm okay. I believe I started this, so stop talking," she said. "Don't do any more thinking either, Dr. Pretty."

A soft laugh rumbled from him. "I wish you'd quit calling me that."

"I can't help it." She ran her hands down his chest and over his stomach until she reached the fly of his jeans and the promising bulge underneath. "Everything about you is so very, very beautiful."

She undid the button and carefully lowered the zipper. He sprang free in her palm, long, hard, and thick. He nudged the cup of her bra aside with his teeth, exposing her breast. His lips tugged at her nipple, sending a tingling jolt through her belly that dampened her panties. She closed her eyes and moaned with pleasure. Her fingers tightened around him and she stroked up and down, again and again, flicking the moistened tip with her thumb until his breath came in raspy gasps. Seconds later, her bra came undone. It fell to the floor.

Her arms and legs trembled. She couldn't remember ever

wanting someone this badly. He had one hand inside her panties, stroking her sensitive folds, dipping a finger inside her until she heard someone begging, only vaguely aware it was her. He grabbed for a condom, ripped it open, and passed it to her. She rolled it over his erection while he peeled her out of her leggings. Then, his hands on her bared bottom, he lifted her into position above him. She braced her knees on the cushioned stool and tried to guide him inside, but he was having none of that.

"Not so fast. I've dreamt about this for days. It's going to last longer than thirty seconds," he ground out, his jaw set with promise. He took control, allowing her only an inch at a time, until she was begging again.

"*Please*, Luke. I can't wait any longer. I want all of you. *Now.*"

The stool skittered backward to bang into the island, as Mara, perched precariously on his thighs and her knees, took him in deep. He withdrew almost to the tip, then thrust upward, again and again, until the ripples of pleasure turned into waves, and her inner muscles began to clench around him. They were both sweating and breathing hard. She arched her back and cried out as she came, his hoarse moans reassuring her that he was coming, too.

The room slowly settled into place. He held her in his arms, which was a good thing. Otherwise, she'd have fallen.

"I have so much to make up for." He groaned, burying his face in her hair. "Although, in my defense, when a woman demands all of me *right now*, I have to oblige."

She was astride him on the stool, her clothes scattered

every which way, his jeans around his ankles. Her damaged knee throbbed, but not unbearably so. He was still inside her, semi hard. Her hair was a tangled mess, she had her cheek pressed into his throat, and she didn't believe she'd ever been this satisfied by a man.

She propped her elbows on his bare chest and kissed him. "Don't worry, Dr. Pretty. I got everything I asked for and more. But if it bothers you, by all means, take all night to perfect your delivery."

THE LOFT WAS dim, lit only by the moon and the stars glowing through the oversized windows. They'd turned off the light in the kitchen before moving to the bed.

Hours had passed. Mara lay naked and boneless on her stomach beside him, her cheek cradled on her folded arms, one softly rounded buttock smooth and warm beneath his palm. Her long, dark mass of hair pooled to one side, exposing her neck. They'd made love three times—each one longer and more exploring than the previous. He couldn't quite believe everything he'd asked of her, or how willing she'd been.

He'd taken her from behind while she'd bent over the back of the sofa that formed one wall of her bedroom. He grew hard again, thinking about the way he'd slid into her, and how she'd bucked against him, raising her hips and crying his name, and the way her tight inner muscles had gripped him as she came.

Then, on the bed, she'd wrapped her long, dancer's legs around his waist and he'd taken his time, easing in and out, tormenting her until she'd again demanded he stop thinking about it and satisfy her.

Sex, simply for the sake of it, was incredible. There was no wondering if it had been good for her, too. She knew what she wanted and wasn't afraid to ask him for it. She'd done everything he'd asked of her, too.

Without hesitation. It had caught him off guard.

He trailed the tip of his finger from the little dimple where the swell of her buttocks began and up the length of her spine. He'd brought her tiger lilies handpicked from his mother's garden because they were the flower that most reminded him of her. She was fire.

He'd let her sleep for a few hours, but he wasn't finished. He couldn't be certain she'd invite him back. Would she be through with him after tonight?

Was this all she wanted from men and why she only dated them once?

"You're thinking again," she admonished without opening her eyes, her voice sex-drugged and sleepy. "Doesn't your brain ever stop?"

"My brain hasn't been driving this bus for the past..." He checked the clock. It was past two in the morning. "*Six hours.*"

He'd redeemed himself. Thank God it was Jake's turn to man the milking parlor in the morning. He'd never notice what time Luke dragged himself home. Zack wasn't as big a concern, since he didn't want to answer any questions, either.

She rolled to her side and propped her head on her hand. "If you ask me if I'm okay with tonight, you can forget about coffee."

The round curve of her breast and its pebbled, dusky pink tip distracted him. "Coffee is the last thing on my mind."

He bent his head and drew it into his mouth, gently sucking, flicking the tip with his tongue. She released a shaky sigh and flipped onto her back, tangling her fingers in his hair, and cradled his head to her breast. One of her legs slid between his. She ran the arch of one foot up and down the back of his calf.

"Oh, my God, that feels good," she breathed.

He moved his mouth to her other breast, then trailed his tongue to her flat belly. Her body was sleek and muscular, although he liked the thin layer of softness that he presumed was thanks to the knee injury restricting her ability to dance. He inched his tongue lower, wondering if she'd finally object. Instead, she lifted her arms above her head and spread her legs open for him. It had been years since a woman had allowed him to do this to her. His first year in university, in fact, when a classmate who'd asked him to tutor her had ended up tutoring him, instead.

His tongue found the swollen nub he was seeking. Mara's breathing shifted to light little pants. He played with the nub, licking and sucking, until she was arching her back, her fingers gripping his head, silently asking for more. He obliged, thrusting his tongue inside her.

"It's not enough," she gasped out. "I need you inside me."

The scent of her—the taste, the way she wriggled her hips—had made him so hard he ached. He grabbed another condom and rolled it on. She pushed him to his back and straddled his hips, taking him so deep inside her she throbbed around his entire erection. He cupped her breasts in his hands as she moved up and down, her palms on his chest, head thrown back. She had her eyes closed, but for his part, he wanted to watch her. She looked like a wild-haired goddess, golden and sleek in the semidarkness.

She went rigid. Her whole body trembled and tightened, and he knew she was close. Just like that, so was he. Heat shot through his groin. She cried out, then collapsed, panting, on top of him. His own release pulsed a little while longer.

When she relaxed, and her breathing become slower and deeper, he withdrew from inside her. Carefully, not wanting to disturb her, he discarded the condom. Then, with her splayed across him and his arms around her, he fell asleep.

He awoke to the smell of coffee and bacon. He was alone in the tangle of sheets.

He rose to his elbows, rubbing the sleep from his eyes. It was quarter past six. Mara was in the sunny kitchen, puttering around in nothing but a pink tank top and pink panties, humming under her breath.

Yes. He watched her. Pink was definitely a girl color, and he couldn't find it in him to object any longer. *Viva la diferencia.*

"Good, you're awake," she called out, all perky and cheerful, clearly a morning person. "Breakfast is ready. I thought you might want to head out early since you've got children waiting for you at home."

He hadn't given a single thought to the kids, or anything but her, since he'd parked his car across the street and knocked on her door. He tried to smother an unwelcome suspicion. Did she really think that, or was she ready for him to leave?

He'd left his clothes on the floor in the kitchen. She'd hung them over the back of the sofa, within reach. He wondered if that was a message. Had he served his purpose and now she was done?

He grabbed his jeans and donned them, leaving the fly open and going commando. He padded barefoot into the kitchen, prepared to help himself to the coffee. Mara scooped bacon from the pan to a plate lined with paper towels. Her hair, a mass of cascading curls, swung round her shoulders when she moved. He could make out the shape of her pretty nipples underneath the tight tank top—one more reason to appreciate pink. And her long legs…

His gaze drifted lower, then stopped. A track of scars ran up her knee to her thigh like railroad ties laid down by a drunk. The flesh was puckered and red. He'd known the scars were there—he'd noticed them last night—but in the dark, and with other things on his mind, he hadn't realized just how badly she'd damaged her leg. His chest tightened. He would have been a lot more considerate if he'd been more aware.

She glanced down to see why he was staring.

"Ugly, right?" She didn't sound at all self-conscious about it.

"That's not what I was thinking. I was thinking I knew you had a bad leg and I should have been more considerate last night."

Her eyes, such a clear, crystal blue against warm, golden skin in the dappled morning light, crinkled up as laughter burst from her. "You made last night all about me. You couldn't possibly have been more considerate."

The guilt abated but didn't quite disappear. "What happened?"

The laughter died and the fire inside her lost some of its *vitalidad*. "A skiing accident," she said, and left it at that.

He considered asking if the skiing accident and her breakup with the pop star whose video she'd danced in were related, but he couldn't see how. A little scar didn't detract at all from the beautiful, sensual, charismatic, *bailarina* she was. Neither did he wish to pursue a subject she seemed unwilling to discuss. He could google it later. It would be his first ever celebrity cyber-stalking.

More importantly, however, they were only sleeping together. Nothing more. He was no expert, but he was willing to bet it didn't give him the right to ask nosy questions.

A bucket of melted ice graced the counter next to the sink, along with two glasses and a bottle of wine with a water-logged label. Another twitch of guilt assailed him. She'd planned more for the evening and he'd rushed things along, because when she'd done that imitation of him and it had been so damned sexy, he'd lost any interest in niceties.

"Grab the coffeepot," she said, carrying the bacon to the tiny dinette set under the window. She'd prepared the table for two. Each plate held a croissant with a bowl of diced fruit beside it. He assumed the metal trivet in the center of the table was for the pot and set the carafe down. The flowers he'd given her perched in a glass vase on the windowsill butting against the table.

They chatted about nothing important while they ate their breakfast. The entire time, Luke wondered what happened next. He was out of practice when it came to casual sex. Had the rules changed? Had this been his one opportunity with her?

His phone pinged. He'd set it on the island last night in case Jake or Zack tried to reach him and forgot all about it. He retrieved it and checked the message. His stomach dropped. It was from Denise.

"Are you ready to come home yet?"

The air turned to ice in his lungs. Did she think they'd had some sort of misunderstanding? Did she think he'd grow *tired* of his family?

He fired a terse text in return. "*I am home.*"

"We need to talk about this."

She'd had her chance. When he'd needed her she hadn't been there for him. "*We said everything that needs to be said before you got on that plane.*"

He tossed the phone on the island with too much force. He couldn't think of anything more awkward than having his fiancée, no matter that she'd walked out on him, calling him at the home of the woman he'd just had fantastic sex with. The phone pinged again, but he ignored it.

Mara set her fork down. "Is everything okay?"

He forced a smile. "Everything's fine. It was no one."

The expression on her face shifted from concern to one of caution, and he replayed what he'd said.

It was no one.

He should have said "nothing," not "no one." Now, he owed her an explanation. "It was my former fiancée. We're no longer together." What a dumb thing to say. That was pretty much what "former" meant.

"She still texts you, though," Mara said. All of her earlier cheerfulness had disappeared.

Damn it, he had no reason to feel guilty.

If only he didn't *sound* so damned guilty, too. "I'm not twelve, Mara. I'm not going to block her. This is the first time she's tried to contact me since we ended our relationship."

"How long since the two of you broke up?" Mara picked up her fork and stabbed a plump cherry, the sharp action belying her serene expression. "Forget I asked. It's none of my business."

He wished he agreed. They might be in this for sex, but he wouldn't be thrilled if the pop star called her right now, either. "We split up shortly after I came to Grand. It turns out she has no interest in kids. Or Montana." Him either, for that matter, other than what he'd represented to her in terms of a lifestyle.

Mara did the math in her head and figured out it had

only been a month. She might like to tease him about being smart, but she wasn't stupid, either.

"I teach a class at eight o'clock," she said.

The clock on the microwave read *7:03*. His heart dropped but he tried to sound cool. "Are you telling me to get out?"

"Not in those exact words." She faked a smile, but it lacked its normal fire.

"Are the exact words, 'Get out and don't ever come back'?"

Gorgeous blue eyes took his measure, and for a moment, the world ceased to turn. Sunlight caught the faint flush spreading across her high cheekbones. Then, she relented. "How about, 'Get out so I can prepare for my class, but you can call me'?"

The world settled back into orbit. He wanted to kiss her, relieved beyond words. If he kissed her, however, he wouldn't stop there, and eight o'clock wasn't that far away.

Besides, he should be getting home. He'd made plans to take Mac and Finn swimming that afternoon, and sooner or later, they'd notice he wasn't on the ranch. Finn, especially, was clingy when people weren't where he thought they should be. His world hadn't yet righted itself and wasn't likely to do so anytime soon.

He downed the last of his coffee. "I'll do that."

Chapter Eight

L UKE TOOK THE boys swimming at the public pool, then for ice cream afterward.

A dry thunderstorm hit as they made their way across the Dairy Queen parking lot to the car. Mac took it in stride. Finn, not so much.

The first streak of lightning didn't spark any major reaction. The second, however—so close it raised all of the fine hairs on Luke's body, and the smell of ozone riddled the air—proved too much for a five-year-old suffering from separation anxiety to ignore, particularly when people began running for cover. Finn attached himself to Luke's leg and refused to let go.

Luke pried him loose and swung him into his arms. "It's okay, bud. I've got you."

He hustled the kids into the car and buckled Finn in his seat. The summer had begun hot and dry and showed no signs of improving. A quick check of the cloudless sky dimmed his hopes. The ranch had cut as much hay as it could, but they'd been holding out for rain. Unless they got some soon the next crop would be a bust, and according to Zack, the ranch needed the money.

By the time he got home the storm had passed without a lick of rain falling, Finn was engaged with Luke's tablet, and Jake was saddling his horse in the yard.

Everyone said Jake and Luke looked alike, but other than the dark hair and green eyes, Luke didn't see it. Jake was a hair shorter, although he had the more muscular build. He didn't smile often, or have much to say, but he had an okay sense of humor that he reserved mostly for family.

"There's smoke out by Camelback Butte," Jake said.

"Want me to come with you?" Luke asked. Lightning strikes often caused grass fires, another setback the ranch didn't need.

"No." He swung into the saddle. "The fire has nowhere to spread and the cattle aren't in any danger. I want to double-check on things is all."

Mac, who'd gotten out of the car, leaned against the hood, his ten-year-old voice filled with hope. "Can I come along?"

Luke knew the answer before Jake even spoke. He also could tell how hard it was for Jake to say no, but safety came first, and Mac couldn't yet sit a horse on his own. They'd also had reports of a bear roaming the area and killing cattle—which was why Jake carried their dad's .338 Winchester Magnum rifle in a scabbard tucked under his knee.

"Not this time, Mac. As soon as you learn to ride though, we'll put you to work. I promise."

"Come on guys," Luke said to the boys. "Go put your wet swim gear in the laundry room and I'll let you play games online."

Offering the boys a chance to use his computer system was an enticement they couldn't resist. He had an ulterior motive, however. He wanted to watch the music video Mara had danced in, and so far today, he'd had no opportunity.

They dropped their towels and swim trunks in the tired washing machine in the mudroom before traipsing through the kitchen, the den, and into a small hallway.

The Wagging Tongue ranch house had been built in the eighteen hundreds, then added to over the decades. The main part of the house had been modernized, but an annex that one of their forefathers had built for aging parents retained much of its rustic charm—heavy emphasis on rustic. It had become more of a guesthouse for extended family visits over the years.

The annex, known as the west wing, had its own outdoor entrance, but it was inconveniently located on the far side of the house where there was no driveway. The easiest way to reach it was through the main part of the building. At one point the McGregors had spoken of taking in paying guests, but Luke's mother hadn't liked the idea of strangers in her home.

Jake had suggested Luke take the space for his own so he could keep his computer equipment away from curious fingers. The wood stove no longer functioned, a small bar fridge sat in a corner, and the kitchen plumbing was crude. A former pantry had been converted to a bathroom with a sink, toilet, and claw-footed tub. Luke had turned the tiny parlor into a computer room, although he used the den in the main house for his home office space so he could help keep an eye on the kids through the day. It lacked the orderliness and clean, modern lines of his apartment in Seattle, but it felt more like home.

He and Denise had talked about moving in together, but they'd both been too busy to make a final decision as to whose apartment they'd keep. They'd both liked having their own space to work in.

There'd been so many signs that things weren't perfect between them, and yet, he'd missed them all.

He set the boys up in the parlor, got them online with the parental controls activated, then took his laptop to the dinette table in the kitchen. The window looked out on the main road, but from his chair he could see the double screens in the other room.

He plugged in his earbuds so the boys couldn't hear what he was up to on his laptop and did a quick search. Stalking a woman online felt a little uncool.

The music video didn't take him long to find. It had one point four billion hits. He watched it twice.

One part in particular captured his attention. Mara's chocolate-brown hair, worn long and loose, flew around her as she spun, head tilted back, arms stretched out wide. Joy lit her face. At one point the camera zoomed in on her smooth, Latina features for a slow motion shot of her lifting her head, then opening her incredible blue eyes to stare into the lens. She made him feel good just by watching.

She made the pop star feel good, too. Jealousy flared. There was no mistaking they had a connection between them. He read a few of the comments before he forced himself to stop. He already knew she had a great ass. He didn't need helpful suggestions as to what he could do with it.

Speaking of asses…

The song was decent. He wasn't much into pop, and the song was sappy as hell, but it didn't make his ears bleed. Little Zee, on the other hand…

His stage name was stupid. He had emo written all over, what with broody dark eyes hidden by black, shaggy hair, pale skin, and a scrawny build that suggested either vampire or crack addict. Luke tried to figure out what Mara had seen in him. Money wasn't her motivator, although the one point four billion hits suggested the money was good.

He couldn't help it. Now that he'd seen the video, he had to check out TMZ and other celebrity sites to get the insider scoop.

What he found wasn't pretty. Mara had been dogged by cameras while still in the hospital, with only the staff to protect her, because Little Zee, the asshole, had left her to fend for herself.

Luke studied the photos. The joy was gone from her face. Her eyes were haunted. And he understood why Diana had taken such an interest in her, and what the dance mothers had meant about her hiding in Grand. People here would have taken one look at her tragic eyes and closed ranks around her, because nosy or not, they were decent.

Now that Little Zee had moved on and Mara was no longer an item of gossip, a lot of the inner joy had come back. She was a survivor, no doubt about that. Luke flipped the lid closed on his laptop and leaned back in his chair. He didn't have far to look to see how resilient people could be. In the other room, Mac was patiently helping Finn work his game controller.

But there was something wrong with a man who could treat a woman that way.

The thought was followed by a spasm of guilt. How, exactly, was the way he treated Mara any better?

Thanks to a poorly-timed text, she'd been very close to telling him she didn't want to see him again. That bothered him. A lot. He couldn't say he was thrilled about the way she'd come into his life, or the timing, but he wasn't sorry she had, and the only reason he wasn't thinking too far ahead right now was because he didn't want to foresee an end. Things were precarious with her and he didn't want to come on too strong.

He'd give her a few days before he called.

Finn bounced into the kitchen. He'd lost interest in playing a game he couldn't quite master and left it to Mac.

"When am I getting my dance stuff?" he asked.

Luke lifted his nephew onto his knee. So far, Finn hadn't blabbed anything to Jake about dancing, which Luke had half expected and been preparing himself for. The fight would be epic.

Finn, however, was too smart for his own good. He played each of his uncles to get what he wanted, and while they knew what he was up to, he was so freaking cute they couldn't resist. It was pretty funny the way he managed to end up sleeping with Jake every night, too.

But he'd also figured out when Jake couldn't be played, and as long as Finn wanted to keep taking dance lessons, then Luke was his go-to.

"How about we go shopping tomorrow afternoon?" Luke suggested. Lydia was growing so fast she could use a few new things, too.

"Mac's game is too hard," Finn complained, eyes wide and beseeching as he moved on to demand number two. "Can I play on your phone?"

The McGregors were trying their best to make things normal and fun for the kids without spoiling them rotten. Luke weighed the importance of winning this battle against giving in from the start, because if he said no he'd have to stand his ground and he didn't have it in him.

"Ten minutes," he said, ceding the flag and handing over the phone. "Then we get cleaned up for supper. What do you say we go out for burgers since Uncle Jake, Uncle Zack, and Lyddie aren't home yet?"

He'd call Mara Tuesday night when she was free. Then, he'd put more effort into the time they spent together. The sex was fantastic, and a big part of the attraction—there was no point in lying—but she deserved more.

NONE OF THE fifteen-year-olds in Mara's Sunday morning jazz class were going to make a career out of dance, but they got a lot of fun out of trying. Three of them were competitive swimmers who used the class as a way to incorporate a different form of exercise into their training program. They said they liked it better than yoga.

Mara turned off the music at the end of the class. The mothers had begun to wander in, eager to see how their daughters compared, even though the girls hated being compared to each other and didn't want to be show ponies. Mara remembered objecting to her mother's presence at dance lessons, too. She'd implemented a no-parent policy early on so her students could express themselves without fear of judgment or face unrealistic expectations at home.

As she spoke with two of the students, she overheard snippets of a conversation near the door. The name "McGregor" was what caught her attention.

"Jake McGregor has Mac in soccer," one woman mused to another. "Interesting, considering Lacey Anderson is the coach. And I heard they were spotted at the Wayside Café, snuggled up by themselves, all deep in 'conversation.'" She used air quotes for emphasis. "They were such a cute couple in high school. Think there's anything more going on?"

"Of course there is. What's equally interesting is that Luke has the younger boy, Finn, taking dance lessons on Saturdays. What are the odds there's something going on between him and Mara, too?"

Mara pretended she hadn't heard, although her face had gotten so hot, no one could possibly be fooled. This wasn't as bad as the whole Little Zee affair, not by a long shot, but still. It was one thing to know people were talking. It was far different to *know*.

"Oh, my God," one of the girls said. She tossed her

blond ponytail and rolled her eyes. "I wish my mom would grow up. Ignore them, Miss Ramos."

"I heard that, Layla," her mother called.

"So did Miss Ramos," Layla fired back. "Who she and Miss Anderson do in their spare time is none of your business."

"Layla!"

The exchange, so inappropriate, had Mara suffering mixed feelings. Part of her thought it was funny. This was what kept her in Grand. The people might be nosy, but their intentions were good. They didn't know everything, however. Neither had she.

And that wasn't funny at all.

She should have known there was a woman in Luke's life. The signs had been there. Mentally, she ticked them off. He hadn't noticed her interest in him when they first met. He had no clue how to flirt. He'd panicked over a kiss that was unexpectedly intense. He'd warned her he wasn't interested in a relationship.

She'd had to do the pursuing.

She'd assumed he was messed up because of the recent tragedy in his family. She'd had a hard, life-altering year herself, and liked not having to make any emotional commitments that might lead to complicated decisions, so she'd thought she understood. The possibility of a fiancée—no matter how former he claimed her to be—hadn't once entered her head.

"It was no one."

The words didn't ring true. Luke was so… family-oriented. If he'd asked someone to marry him, then he'd been deeply committed, and a month wasn't enough time for him to recover, especially not when he was also dealing with grief. What if the breakup was temporary? What if he went back to her? What was she like?

What if he still loved her?

He wasn't yet free. That text had confirmed it.

Tell him it's time to move on.

That was what she should have done the moment she found out about the fiancée. A sexual relationship between two consenting adults was one thing. She didn't want to be the other woman. The third wheel. The mistress.

The one less important.

She really didn't want all of Grand knowing it, either.

The phone finally rang Tuesday night.

She hugged her knees as she sat on the sofa—the same one she'd clung to as he'd given her the second of four heart-stopping orgasms—and let the phone ring three times. The stars were coming out in the navy-blue sky. She gazed up at them through the window.

Then, on the fourth ring, she answered.

"Hey," Luke said. "I hope I didn't make you run for the phone."

His concern for her came through the connection, gliding warm hands over her skin, and for a moment, Mara stopped breathing. No sane woman would give up a man like this without a fight.

"No," she said.

"I see." She could picture his dark-lashed, green eyes narrowing as he figured out that she'd let the phone ring because she couldn't decide whether or not to pick up. "I'm coming over." It wasn't a question.

"Maybe another night. I'm tired and I have a headache," she lied.

"I won't stay long. I forgot my hat." There was another pause. "I think we should talk."

"Meaningful conversation isn't really my forte," she said, then wondered where that had come from. She'd traveled extensively. She wasn't uneducated. It wasn't Dr. Pretty's fault that he made her think of nothing but sex when she was with him.

She'd liked it that way.

"Is that what's bothering you? You think we can't talk on the same level?"

Yes.

She was as surprised by the discovery as he seemed to be. Thinking about the kind of woman he'd been willing to commit to had intimidated her, and she wasn't used to that.

"I have interests other than my work," he said. His tone had changed. She heard relief. *Is that all the problem is?* "I enjoy your company, Mara. You're easy to be around. You're not just a dreamer—you're also a doer. That's a rare combination."

She needed to do something right now, before things moved in a direction she hadn't intended. She would have been fine with them being friends instead of lovers, but they couldn't be both. Now, she wasn't sure they could have been either of those.

She'd been quiet too long.

"You're thinking too hard," he said. "Why can't we just continue to enjoy ourselves without worrying about what happens tomorrow?"

She had to smile at having her own words thrown back at her. She wished she didn't *like* him so much. "Has anyone ever told you that you can be a jerk?"

"I have two brothers and a ten-year-old nephew. I hear that every day." The line crackled a little. "This is about the text I got, isn't it?"

"It threw me a little," she admitted. "I'm not okay with you being involved with someone else."

"I'm not. I swear to you, Mara—we've split up and we're not getting back together. I'm coming over," he said again.

She found her voice. "Not tonight." And then, because she wanted to believe him, and was suddenly terrified of never seeing him again, she heard herself blurt out, "How about Saturday night, instead?"

"I can't. It's Jake's evening off. Zack and I are manning the ranch and the kids." His voice lowered, growing husky. "I really want my hat back, though. What's your schedule like for next Tuesday?"

Say you're busy.

She stared up at the night sky brim full of stars shining through glass. She'd started this. She wasn't changing the rules on him, or letting him change them on her. A year from now, she didn't know where she might be. If the dance studio didn't take off by then, she'd need to re-evaluate her situation. If he went back to his fiancée and his former life once his time in Montana was over, then that was on him.

How she dealt with the gossip would be up to her.

She'd held her head high once before and survived.

"Wide open," she said.

Chapter Nine

Luke brushed the tips of his fingers along the length of Mara's spine, admiring the feel of her skin.

She lay on her stomach, her face toward him, her arms folded under her cheek. Moonlight turned her into a naked Mayan goddess. Her eyes were closed, although she wasn't asleep. Long lashes fluttered, making him wonder what her thoughts were.

He could lie here and watch her for hours, and never grow tired.

This was the fourth time in the three weeks since they'd started sleeping together that he'd spent at least part of the night. He'd gotten into the habit of going home before dawn, mostly because they had a ten-year-old in the house who was wise for his age, and the brothers worried about setting the right kind of example for him.

"You're staring," Mara said, without opening her eyes.

"Does it bother you?"

"No." She flipped onto her back and stretched her arms over her head, opening her eyes to gaze up at him. His fingers trailed over the firm mound of one breast and she caught her breath. The night was warm. They'd kicked the sheets to the foot of the bed and she tucked her toes underneath them. "What are you thinking about?"

He said the first thing that popped into his head. "Why does everyone in Grand seem to believe you don't date?"

Her eyebrows went up. "What makes you think everyone's right?"

"They don't have their facts straight most of the time," Luke conceded. He stroked her flat belly, watching the way her muscles tightened beneath his touch. "Although you've got to admit, they usually aren't that far off base. We've only gone out in public once, yet we're sleeping together."

She was watching him closely. "What conclusions are you drawing from that?"

"I'm not sure." He'd arrive. He'd kiss her. And the next thing he'd know, they were in bed. He wasn't worried that they weren't exclusive. She'd never given him any reason to doubt that they were. Besides, he'd have heard the rumors during his coffee dates with the dance mothers if other men had been hanging around, expressing an interest. But he couldn't seem to get her to talk anymore and it was driving him nuts. "There's a distinct possibility I'm fitting into a pattern," he said.

She arched a brow. "Does it matter if you are?"

It really did. The sex was great. Better than great. When he kissed her he couldn't think, and in all honesty, his brain had needed the break.

But his brain couldn't be entirely shut off forever. It said he'd had just as great a time with her at Reality Bytes, and wanted more of that from her, too. It also warned him that, if the pattern proved true, she eventually lost interest in men. She was—or had been—all about dance.

"We'd agreed we aren't going to think about the future," she reminded him, as if reading his thoughts. She shifted to face him, resting one slender hand on his hip.

"We did. So let's talk about the past, instead."

He felt a subtle tensing in her fingers. A slight shift in her mood. She was no longer so languid.

"You first," she said. "Tell me about your fiancée. When you met, what attracted you to her?"

She'd thrown down a challenge. She didn't expect him to do it.

And he didn't want to. Denise deserved her privacy. He didn't want to think about her, either. What he had with Mara was different, and what he felt for her was, too. But he couldn't help thinking he might have a lot riding on this, so he picked his words with care.

"She was so self-confident," he said. "She challenged a paper I wrote on natural language processing and cloud communication."

"I have no idea what you just said."

"Why should you? You don't work in the field. I didn't know what a swish split was, either, until I met you."

Her lips curved. "You've been doing your homework."

"Of course. If it's important to you, then I want to know about it."

She digested that. "Fair warning. I am never going to read your paper on cloud processing or whatever."

"I don't expect you to. You didn't need to build the platform for virtual reality games in order to enjoy playing them, did you? I'm never going to be a dancer either, but I can still appreciate the performance."

"You really are smart," she said.

"Does that mean you'll stop calling me Dr. Pretty?"

"No." She touched his face, then traced the seam of his lips with one fingertip. "You're still so very beautiful, too."

"I'm starting to think you only want me for my body." He wished he could take those words back when she didn't deny them. She didn't believe they had anything in common other than sex. He took her hand and rolled off the bed, dragging her with him. "Come on, then. If that's the case, then we might as well put it to good use."

He led her hand in hand through the apartment, both of them naked, and didn't stop when they reached the door, but instead, pulled it open.

"Where are we going?" Mara asked, allowing him to draw her onto the catwalk.

"You'll see."

He held her hand on the stairs. An emergency light over the door in the studio cast a faint red glow that bounced off the mirrored walls and into the far corners of the room. He fumbled with the sound system, selecting the track he wanted. The strains of a Lou Bega mambo drifted into the room.

"No, Luke," she said, trying to free her hand from his when she figured out his intentions.

Rather than let her go, he tugged her toward him. "Yes, Mara."

She pressed her forehead against his chest. "I can't dance a mambo."

She wanted to, though. He'd seen the longing in her expression as the music began. And there were plenty of things his body was good for other than sex.

"Neither can I. But I bet we can do it together if you walk me through it." He turned her around so her back was to his front, her bare ass nestled against his thighs, her hair caught between her shoulders and his chest. He was reminded of the night at Reality Bytes, and how much he'd enjoyed this particular position. She'd trusted him then. He saw no reason why she shouldn't now. He brushed her hair aside and nuzzled the length of her throat with his lips. "The trick is to let me carry your weight," he murmured against her skin.

"I take back what I said about you being smart."

But already, she'd begun to move to the beat of the music. Luke put his hands on her hips, supporting her body, allowing her movements to guide his. It took her a few steps to get used to leaning against him, the two of them dancing as one. His part was easy. All he had to do was follow her lead, keeping one thigh in close contact with her weaker side so she couldn't stumble.

They danced for two songs before Mara twisted to face him, flinging her arms around his neck. He held her by the waist and she tipped her head back, closing her eyes. When she opened them to gaze up at him, even in the dim studio lighting he could recognize the same soft look of joy she'd worn in the music video. His heart clenched tight with longing. He wanted her so badly. Much more of her than she'd been willing to give him so far.

He wanted her wearing that look for him.

"Thank you," she said. "This was wonderful."

He lifted her, bearing her weight on his arms. She wrapped her legs around his hips and took his face in her hands, bending her head to kiss him. She slid her tongue into his mouth. He carried her to the barre, positioned himself between her parted thighs, and eased his erection inside her.

He wasn't wearing a condom. He began to withdraw, but Mara clamped her knees around his hips.

"I use birth control and I had a physical six weeks ago," she assured him, panting the words around soft little moans. Already, tiny muscles had begun to tighten around him. She was close.

So was he.

"I've only had one other partner in more than five years," he thought she said. He couldn't be sure. Pinpoints of light prickled the backs of his eyes. He braced his feet a little farther apart and thrust again and again, faster and deeper, half afraid he might hurt her, he was so eager, but she didn't protest.

She arched her back, her fingers biting into his shoulders, greeting each of his strokes with small cries of encouragement. She'd anchored her heels against the backs of his knees.

"Look at me," he said. He wanted to watch her face—to see her expression—to find out what he did to her, and if it was even close to what she did to him.

She opened brilliant, heavy-lidded blue eyes. It was the biggest turn-on he'd ever experienced. Her whole body stiffened, clenched muscles quivering around him, and he groaned with sheer bliss as they came at the same time to the beat of mambo music.

"This was wonderful, too," she whispered against his throat. He hadn't yet withdrawn, reluctant to end the intimacy between them. She made him feel whole—as if his world, which had been torn apart, had pulled itself back together. The pieces might be different, but nonetheless, it was complete.

He didn't dare say so to her.

They managed to make it back to her bed, where he draped a possessive arm around her and held her against him. As good as it had been, something was still missing.

He'd seen desire in her eyes. He'd seen pleasure.

He was determined he'd see joy, too.

SATISFACTION COURSED THROUGH her veins. She'd been right to assume he was a natural dancer. He was a natural lover, too.

She'd never danced completely naked before, let alone with a partner. It wasn't an activity she would ever have thought of on her own. Yet Luke had been so unselfconscious about combining the two activities. There was nothing about the human body that he wasn't comfortable with. He didn't mind her scarred leg either, other than concern as to whether or not it caused her discomfort.

She didn't care about scars or a little physical discomfort. For a whole year, being unable to dance the more basic steps, and knowing she'd never perform in public again, had been less important to her than where her next paycheck would come from.

How had he known what she wanted—what she'd *needed*—when she hadn't known it, herself?

Tonight, despite her intentions, they'd broken the rules. They'd gone beyond sex. Friendship too, for that matter. And she dared to hope that maybe he hadn't been as invested in his fiancée as she'd assumed. Maybe the fiancée had been a mistake and it had taken a tragedy for him to realize it. He'd broken up with her before Mara had entered the picture.

The unsteady rhythm of his chest rising and falling against her back and shoulders said he was awake. It was very late though, and soon, he'd be leaving. He'd only ever spent the one night.

She didn't want him to go.

"Stay with me," she said.

The arm around her tightened. He kissed the top of her head. "I'd love to. It's hard to crawl out of a warm bed." She heard regret and the "but" that was coming. "But Finn loses his mind if he wakes up and we aren't there. And Mac isn't stupid. He knows what it means when his uncles don't come home until the next morning. We need to set a good example for him in the way we treat women. I don't want him to hit sixteen or seventeen and think casual sex is okay."

The statement about casual sex stung—even though it was what they were engaged in. She'd been the one to insist.

"At what age does it become okay?" she asked.

Suddenly, she was on her back underneath him and he was propped on his elbows, his face above hers. Dark brows pinched together. Moonlight made his frown more intense. "There's *nothing* casual about this."

She closed her eyes, the relief overwhelming. She should tell him he was wrong. That this was why she'd only dated men in Grand once or twice—they became too possessive, and she'd learned her lesson about that. She'd been nothing more than a possession to Little Zee, and never again.

But Luke wasn't Little Zee. He wasn't quite like any of the men in Grand she'd dated either, although the qualities that had attracted her to them were there. He was solid and honest.

No matter how much she wanted to, she found it very hard to believe that he could have gotten over his fiancée so quickly.

"Did you love her?" she asked.

Despite the turn in the conversation, he knew who she meant. "I thought I did. But you learn a lot about people when push comes to shove. Did you love the pop star?" he asked in return.

Someone had filled him in on the story. Either that or he'd looked it up when he'd done his research on dance. It was a piece of her life that she couldn't keep private, but she'd managed to keep how she'd felt to herself.

She'd had a year and a half to recover, not a month,

however, so he had no right to compare their situations.

"No," she said. "I loved dance and he loved music, and when we worked on the video together, that spilled over into a physical relationship. We both knew it wouldn't last." She'd chosen to enjoy it while it did, so that was on her. She'd never expected to have him leave her so abruptly, and with such a complete indifference for her well-being, however. The selfish bastard. "This won't last, either."

"How do you know it won't?" Luke settled more comfortably, bearing his weight with his elbows. The crisp hairs on his legs chafed the smooth skin of her thighs. "We agreed we weren't going to think too far ahead, so unless you have a crystal ball, you don't know where this will end up. One thing it's not, however, is casual. We both know that, whether or not you're willing to admit it." He kissed her throat. It seared like a brand. "But a ten-year-old doesn't have the same understanding of the situation. No one else does. This is between you and me."

She loved that he thought about what was best for Mac first. He was good with Finn, too. And to dance with her the way he had...

She wanted so much to trust him. To believe he knew his own heart.

"You're right. It's not casual," she said. Her chest palpitated like crazy. She hadn't expected for them to become this involved. "I'm not sure I understand what's going on between us either, though. So why don't you explain it to me?"

"I think we were both lost, and we've found each other

in a place where we were both meant to be."

"Interesting theory, Dr. McGregor. I had no idea you minored in astrology."

Luke ran his finger along her lower lip. "Scoff if you will. You've bought top-of-the-line appliances and you redid the kitchen. Your furniture is new. You installed a sound system and painted the walls. And yet, according to the ladies I have coffee with every Saturday morning, you aren't yet turning a profit. Why spend so much money turning this warehouse into a home unless this is where you belong?"

The psychoanalysis made her uncomfortable. She really had spent too much money. "Don't read too much into it. When I was growing up, the first thing my mother did when we'd arrive in a new city was to turn whatever we were renting into a home for us. She calls it a nesting instinct. As a dancer, I've never been in one place for longer than a few months. It was fun to make a home for myself. I had some savings, so I thought it was time to give it a try."

She'd needed a hideout. A haven. A place where she could recover without the world staring, waiting for her to crack. Grand was hardly private, but no one here had ever shown her anything but kindness. The O'Sullivans sprang to mind.

"What does your mother think of your efforts? Does she like Montana?"

"She hasn't seen it," Mara said.

Luke ceased his one-fingered exploration of the curves of her face. He blinked. His expression was priceless. "Your home? Or Montana? She didn't come here to be with you after your accident?"

Mara loved her mother, but while she was more reserved than her Mexican in-laws, she possessed a great deal of Dutch forthrightness and there'd been too strong a probability of her publicly expressing her opinion of Little Zee. Mara wouldn't give him the free publicity. She wouldn't give the paparazzi any more access to her life, either.

"I told her the press made a big deal about nothing," Mara said. "She volunteers at an orphanage in Brazil and I thought the children would benefit more from her attention. You can understand that."

"I get it. But my mother would have killed me if I'd had career-ending surgery and pretended it was nothing."

Career-ending.

A part of her brain flinched. Hearing it spoken out loud made it sound so... final. So real. She was only twenty-six. She had so many years ahead of her. She longed to argue that there'd been a mistake, but she shook off the urge. Her argument was weak and there was no need to prove it.

"Which is why mine will never know," she said. The hint of envy when Luke mentioned his mother made her realize how lucky she was to have hers. Also, that the topic of conversation needed to change. "Tell me why you were lost. I got the impression you love to teach."

"I do. I don't necessarily love to teach in Seattle."

That came as a surprise. They were both learning new things about each other. "You'd give up your position to come home to Montana? Could you find something similar here?"

"Now we're talking about the future. That's not allowed." Luke sat up. He stroked his flat palm over her naked belly, his touch filled with reluctance. He stood, and reached for his jeans on the floor by the bed. "I've got to go."

It seemed neither one of them was ready to talk about where their lives might be headed.

She donned a robe and followed him through the apartment to the kitchen door. The light over the stove cast a warm yellow glow. She'd given him a key to the main door—at his request—so she wouldn't have to go up and down the stairs to let him in or lock up behind him. This was the third time he'd used it. Always, however, he texted her before he came over.

He was so thoughtful.

She told him one more secret. It was the closest she'd ever come to telling a man he was special. "I've never given anyone else a key to my home, before."

He had one shoe on. He crammed his socks in his pocket. Black eyelashes shuttered his thoughts, although emotion was thick in his manner. "You aren't getting it back."

He kissed her goodbye and she closed the door. She listened for his footsteps descending the rickety stairs, then the muffled sound of his car engine starting on the far side of the quiet street.

She wasn't ready to go back to bed. She got herself a glass of water, then, with one hand on the kitchen counter for balance, hummed a few bars of mambo and danced a few steps. How had he known what to do for her? What she'd like?

She knew so little about him.

What could she do for him in return?

SHE'D GIVEN HIM her key, which was now priceless to him, and begun to question what their relationship—or lack of one—was.

Meaning she hadn't loved the pop star. The asshole. Thank God.

Because Luke couldn't compete with fame and fortune.

A heart-to-heart about the future at three in the morning probably wouldn't have netted the results either one of them sought, however.

The scent of hydrangea riddled the air, and as he stepped into the night, closing and locking the front door firmly behind him, he breathed it in deep. He turned his phone on once he was in the car. He'd gotten into the habit of shutting it down when he was with Mara. He had two brothers. They didn't all need to be on call for the kids.

He found a new text.

"Enough Luke. You've had two months. We HAVE to talk."

Luke sighed, rubbed the back of his neck, and started the car. Maybe they did. Denise was nothing if not persistent. She'd made up her mind and she wouldn't give up. He'd once found that single-minded focus attractive.

So many things in his life had changed. No matter what happened with the ranch, he wasn't going back to Seattle. Montana was home.

He found Zack, fully dressed, in the kitchen, sitting at the table drinking a mug of hot chocolate. Yellow curtains fluttered over the sink. The windows were open wide in a futile attempt to cool off the inside of the house before the rising sun brought back its blistering heat. A series of loud chirps, peeps, and croaks announced the presence of a northern mockingbird somewhere outside in the night.

"What are you doing still up?" Luke asked.

Zack widened innocent eyes over the rim of his mug. "How come you're just getting in?"

They were back to this game.

Luke drew up a chair across from Zack and rested clasped hands on the table. "Got a question for you."

"Yes. You look ridiculous when you wear that stupid cowboy hat. This isn't a dude ranch."

"Duly noted." He bounced his clasped fists up and down. He couldn't believe he was about to ask his brother this question, but it wasn't as if he could discuss it with Mara. "When you say to a woman, 'If you walk out that door, we're finished,' what do you think she really hears?"

Zack set the mug down. "Is it the same woman who didn't stick around for a memorial service for our parents?"

"Yes."

Blue eyes narrowed. "Then I don't give a damn what she heard. All that matters is whether or not you meant what you said."

Luke had meant it. He didn't like this sense of unfinished business hanging over him, however. It was affecting Mara now, too. On the surface she seemed to have everything together. Underneath, he wasn't as sure.

"Thanks," Luke said. "I'll let Jake know too, but I'm going to Seattle for a few days. I've got to pack up my apartment and arrange to teach some online classes next year."

"As long as you stick to your guns while you pack," Zack said, sipping his cocoa. "She might be hard of hearing, in which case you'll have to repeat yourself once or twice."

Her hearing was fine. It was simply selective.

Luke booked a flight before going to bed.

Then, he sent Mara a text.

"I'll be out of town for a few days on business. I'll call when I get back."

Chapter Ten

SEATTLE WAS GREEN in the summer. Lush western hemlock, red cedar, and well-tended shrubs limned the parkways and streets.

It was the cold, dreary, sunless winters that began in late fall and didn't let up until April or May that Luke truly disliked. He'd always been in a classroom or computer lab so he hadn't realized how much he missed Montana's crisp blue skies and sparkling mantles of snow.

He'd get to enjoy winter this year. He could teach Mac and Finn how to ski. They'd take Lydia sledding with them. The ranch had snowmobiles, too. In a year or so, Mac would be old enough for dirt biking—depending on whether or not old mother hen Jake stopped all the fussing.

And there would be Mara. He'd bring her out to the ranch. He'd teach her to drive a tractor and how to ride a horse. They'd play more virtual reality games together and she could teach him to dance. He'd help her see how much Grand had to offer. She was half in love with it now.

He cut the rental car into the crowded lot across from the Japanese Garden off Lake Washington Boulevard East and parked under a shady tree.

He strolled a stone path that wound around a quiet pond until he came to the bench where they'd agreed to meet. It was partially hidden by carefully-positioned greenery. Turned earth, blooming flowers, and red cedar intertwined scents.

The garden was a popular spot. He'd brought his laptop here many times on sunny days to get away from the four walls of his office. He'd asked Denise to meet him here because it was one of his favorite places to sit and relax. It always put him at ease.

It was also public, but gave an illusion of privacy, because this conversation wasn't going to be easy. He planned to tell her about Mara, too. He'd already packed up his apartment and given his notice. He'd spoken to the college and arranged his online workload for the next year. He didn't have to give them any definite decision until December, but he knew what his decision would be. Nothing came before family.

It wasn't long before Denise approached. She walked briskly, not looking around, focused entirely on her objective. She'd tucked short, dark-blond hair, cut in a bob, behind her ears. Tall and slender, she was pretty. Beautiful, even.

But in a contained manner. There was no fire to her. When he looked in her eyes, which were a clear, almost gray shade of blue, he couldn't tell what she was thinking. In the beginning, that had intrigued him. It lent an air of mystery to her.

There was no mystery, however. She was all about

work—his as well as hers. College life had kept them together. The first test to take them into the real world, and life's ugly realities, had torn them apart.

He'd never be able to forget how she hadn't supported him. All the guilt that had niggled at the back of his mind disappeared. Even without Mara, they were through.

She sat beside him on the bench. "I heard you were on campus this morning. Why didn't you come to my office, rather than make both of us drive all the way here?"

"I like it here," Luke said.

"So do I. But it's hardly a practical place to hold a private conversation. At least in my office we could have closed the door." Denise sighed, rubbing her knees in a gesture that signaled frustration. "The last time I tried to talk to you, you wouldn't listen."

What had she expected from him? They'd been in his parents' home, disposing of their belongings, and he'd been trying to prepare rooms for three orphaned children. He'd been numb.

"I could say the same thing about you," he said.

"I'm listening now. Go ahead."

"I've met someone else."

That wasn't how he'd intended to start this conversation. The words simply escaped.

Shock flared in Denise's eyes before it was carefully sucked in and contained. She struggled for a few moments, as if searching for the right response to a situation completely foreign to her.

He waited.

"I understand," she finally said. "We can get past this."

He hadn't expected that. He supposed he should have. "There's nothing to get past. I asked you to spend a year in Grand with me and my family, and instead, you walked out the door."

"You're a smart man. I wanted to give you time to come to your senses. It was too much of your brother to ask. We'd be giving up on two careers, not one. It simply didn't make sense when Jake already had Zack there to help out. Why does it take three grown men to look after three children? Grand has childcare options, doesn't it?"

Denise sounded truly bewildered. She had no concept of family. She was an only child to parents who'd had her late in life and they catered to her. Luke, too, had constantly given in whenever they had differing opinions—because they'd never had any differences he'd believed worth arguing about. Not until now.

He rubbed his forehead with his fingertips. He was as much to blame for their failed relationship as she was. He'd never fully understood how spoiled she was. He'd be wasting his breath to try and explain that neither he nor his brothers knew anything about traumatized children, or parenting in general, and that there was a family business to run. Not to mention, they had their own losses to deal with.

A black-haired toddler ran past, followed by an indulgent older man who was no doubt his grandfather. The toddler looked to be around Lydia's age. Denise never spared him a glance.

"I've given the college my notice," Luke said. "I won't be

coming back to Seattle."

"You're making a mistake." Unshed tears glittered in Denise's eyes. Anger spilled over instead, hot and bitter and thick. "I hope she's worth it. Because that's what this is really about."

He'd handled this badly. He shouldn't have started by bringing up Mara because this wasn't about her at all. It wasn't about her unwillingness to come to Grand with him, either. At the end of the day, it was about two people who'd been on the verge of making a terrible mistake. The marriage would never have lasted.

"No," Luke said. "It's not about Mara. You and I were done the day you left Grand, and you know it. I told you about her only because I want you to know I've moved on and I think you should, too."

"I can't move on," Denise said. She started to cry, soundlessly, fat tears dripping from her lower lashes to slide down her cheeks. "I'm pregnant."

LUKE SAID HE would call, but it had been almost two weeks.

Mara tried not to read too much into it, especially when his younger brother Zack brought Finn to his dance lesson on Saturday morning—and then the next Saturday, too. Luke also missed their date Tuesday night.

It wasn't like him not to at least send her a text if he had to cancel. She'd thought about calling him, but that wasn't how things worked between them.

Her track record for misjudging men remained intact. She should have known better than to fall for "*There's nothing casual about this.*"

The studio was warm this morning. She wedged a piece of wood under the front door to prop it open and allow fresh air to flow through. She'd installed a water cooler for her students, but insisted the younger children each bring a full plastic sports bottle to class. They liked to play with the cooler, meaning they had to drink water first if they wanted to refill their bottles from it. Hydration kept their muscles from cramping.

The students began trickling in. Three of the girls sat on the floor in their leotards and tights, exchanging sandals for dance shoes. Shortly before class was to start, Finn darted into the studio ahead of his uncle. He wore the form-fitting T-shirt and bike shorts she'd recommended, as well as white ankle socks with his flats. One front tooth was missing. He was so sweet.

Finn looked how Zack McGregor must have as a child. Zack was another beautiful man, proof that the McGregors had won some sort of Irish gene pool lottery. Zack and Luke had similar features, although their coloring was different. Zack had red hair that bordered on brown and his eyes were blue, not green.

Zack didn't have Luke's dancer's grace, however, and whereas Luke was quiet and oblivious to female attention, Zack soaked it up. Age was no barrier to him and his charms, either. He was a natural flirt. He knew the name of each little girl in Finn's class, and spoke a kind word to each one, earning him the adoration of their mothers, too. Mara was glad Zack had sent Luke to the store for fennel, or she might have hooked up with the wrong McGregor.

Lydia straddled Zack's hip with her thumb in her mouth. According to Luke she was now twenty-two months old. A definite observer, inclined to assess her surroundings and everyone in them before making any commitments, she was as cute as her brother. She owned the same long-lashed green eyes. Fluffy blond hair that couldn't make up its mind as to what color it planned to be stood straight up on end.

Mara wished she could ask Zack where Luke was.

One of the mothers saved her the trouble. "What happened to Luke? He usually brings Finn to class."

"Working in the fields and in the barn today," Zack replied. "I drew the kids and the cooking. Mostly because nobody else would tackle the cooking."

Which meant he was home and deliberately avoiding her. She felt so stupid. At least with Little Zee the accident had explained it.

This time she had nothing.

"Life is rough, Cinderella," a mother named Cossette said. She lived on a ranch and knew all the ranchers, as well as their gossip. "I heard a rumor you take Lydia next door for diaper changes."

"That's not why I heard he goes next door," the first mother mused, soliciting laughs. When it subsided, "Are you and Lydia joining us for coffee this morning, Zack?" she asked.

"Why? So you can quiz us about Posey Davies?" He consulted his niece. "Do we look crazy, Lyds?"

"So Mara doesn't have another McGregor looking for private dance lessons after hours," Cossette said.

Heat crawled beneath Mara's skin, from her neck to her face, where it burned hot enough to leave her light-headed. In her imagination, she heard Lou Bega's mambo. Luke's body was against hers, his arms holding her tight as they swayed to the music.

How had everyone in Grand found out about that?

"And because we want to get to know Lydia, too," Felicity, another member of the dance morning coffee klatch, chimed in. She lifted the little girl out of Zack's arms. "She looks just like Liz. Don't you, sweetie?"

Lydia was now the center of attention and seemed uncertain as to how much she intended to tolerate. She examined Felicity with wide eyes, then apparently decided she liked what she saw, because she didn't object to the exchange. Felicity, a doctor, really knew how to handle wee patients.

Mara came back to earth. The women were only joking with Zack—but the damage was done. He had to be well aware that Luke stayed out late on certain nights. The way his gaze lingered on her guilty face, and the dawning light in his eyes, said he now knew with whom.

"Okay, everyone," she called out to the children, clapping her hands to cut through the noise and attract their attention. It was also the adults' signal to leave because class was about to begin. "Let's start our warm-ups."

She was too busy for the next hour to think too much about either of the McGregor brothers. By the time class was over, she'd decided she was overreacting. Luke went away on business. He came home. Work at the ranch, plus caring for three children, had overwhelmed him.

Maybe he'd decided casual worked best for him, after all. If so, she couldn't expect him to always be as considerate as he had been to now.

The last little girls waved goodbye as they followed their mothers outside, leaving Mara facing Luke's brother, who'd lingered behind. Lydia was confident enough with her surroundings that she stood on her own at his side, although she clung tightly to one of his fingers.

"Can I speak to you for a moment?" Zack asked Mara.

He sounded so serious. Her heart skipped a beat. Bad news was coming. Had something happened to Luke? Was that why he hadn't called?

"Of course." She had no idea what Luke might have told him about her. Or if he'd said anything at all. She couldn't decide which she'd prefer. She forced a smile to her lips and played dumb. "Your nephew is very talented, as I'm sure you're already aware."

Zack gently pried his finger free of Lydia's grip. "Go play with Finn," he said to her.

The little girl waddled off to join her brother, who was practicing third position in front of the barre. Her diaper-clad bottom bobbed up and down as she aped his movements. Watching them together was too cute for words.

Sharp blue eyes scanned Mara from head to toe. Then, Zack cut to the chase. "Do you have any idea why Luke's been in a funk ever since he got back from Seattle?"

She heard one thing. "Luke went to Seattle?" She tried to make sense out of that. He'd told her he was going out of town on business. But if it was business, why hadn't he simply said where he was going?

"You didn't know?" A hint of doubt softened the hard edge of Zack's accusing tone.

"I haven't seen him since last Tuesday."

A sick sensation crawled through her stomach. Between now and then, something had happened. He had been fine when he left her apartment. Then, a few hours later, he'd sent her a text saying he had to go out of town on business for a few days.

His business had been in Seattle. She didn't like where this was going.

"Maybe I should mind my own business," Zack said. Now he was uneasy, too. Whatever he'd blamed her for, he now saw his mistake. "If Luke ever asks, I don't suppose we could pretend this conversation never took place?"

Before they did that, she had a few questions of her own. She stared at the children to avoid looking at Zack. Finn had third position down pat, but needed to work on how he held his hands. Lydia, who'd grown bored thanks to her brother's lack of interest in her, was chattering to herself in one of the mirrors. She pressed her nose and mouth against the glass and laughed at the distortion it made.

"When did Luke get back from Seattle?" Mara asked Zack.

"I'm going to be in so much trouble," he said. Awkwardness stretched between them. "Maybe you should give him a call."

Maybe she should. She'd been tossed aside once without any warning and she deserved better than that. Especially from Luke, who'd pretended they had something more.

Something she'd begun to want.

She beat her anger back through sheer force of will. Her last breakup had been too public for her to have any say. Letting her rage out then would have hurt no one but herself. She'd had nothing to gain.

This time was different.

"I'll do that," she said.

"When you do, can you tell him to quit being such a huge pain in the ass?" Zack asked.

THE NUMBERS ON the screen no longer made any sense. Luke rubbed his eyes under his glasses. He was tired. He'd driven a tractor all afternoon, fixed a sensor on one of the robots, and he had another hour-long online tutorial coming up.

Also, the fields were ready for mowing, which meant between that, the cattle, and the biomass power plant, they'd be going flat out for the next month at least. So much for August. Jake had a young crew of local teenagers hired on to help out, but they required adult supervision.

Right now, Lydia was next door with Posey and the boys were out on the patio off the family room so Luke could keep an eye on them while he worked. The outer glass doors were open. He could see Finn practicing his dance steps. Mac was on the grass where he had Thunder—the young foal Jake had bought him and allowed him to name—on a lead rope, teaching him to respect personal space the way Jake had shown him he should. Mac loved that foal. He'd make a rancher someday.

And as far as being a dad went, Jake was shaping into a natural.

Zack poked his head into Luke's office. "Got a minute?"

Luke looked at the time. "I have ten of them. What's up?"

Zack lifted a stack of books off a wooden chair and sat down. He looked at the ceiling, as if in silent prayer, then at Luke. "I talked to Mara today."

Luke took off his glasses, folded them, and set them down. He rubbed his eyes again, mostly to hide his reaction to hearing her name. He was too tired to keep playing this game of pretend with his brother. "What did she say?"

"That you haven't called her since you came back from Seattle."

He'd tried to. At least fifty times. And he'd have to talk to her sooner or later, but he'd been having a hard time getting his head back together. He didn't know what to say—not to her, nor to his brothers. He didn't know how to tell Jake and Zack that at the end of the summer, he'd have to leave.

He was going to be a father.

He didn't believe he'd be a natural at it, either. Not the way Jake was. And his child would never know ranch life the same way he hoped Liz's kids would.

He'd had his whole year planned. Now, his plans were in shambles. He'd also have to look for a new job in Seattle, because he'd refused to withdraw his written notice to the college. Denise had been furious about it, but since she wouldn't reconsider a move to Montana so he could be part of the pregnancy too, he didn't care. Maybe that was why he'd refused.

It wasn't fair to Denise that she should have to go through a pregnancy alone, however. She hadn't asked for this any more than he had, and he should be there for her, even though she'd made it clear that right now she was happy to have some distance between them.

Mara carried equal weight in his thoughts. He missed her so much that he ached. He didn't want to hurt her. He really didn't want to lose her.

"There's nothing casual about this."

There wasn't. But his current situation wasn't something he could talk to her about. *"Guess what? That former fiancée I swore to you I was done with? Turns out she's pregnant."*

The responsibility was his.

"I take it things didn't go the way you expected," Zack added, when Luke didn't speak. "Did you change your mind about Denise? Are you two back together?"

"She's pregnant," Luke said.

Shock bleached Zack's face white. He opened his mouth, but it took a few tries for him to get any words out. "Are you sure it's yours?"

"It's mine." He had no doubts about that. Denise

wouldn't cheat.

He'd always thought he wouldn't, either.

He *hadn't*.

"When is she due?" Zack asked.

"Early February."

Meaning she'd gotten pregnant in May, right around when he'd received word of the plane crash. He'd used sex to burn off his grief and she'd used it so they wouldn't have to discuss a move to Montana. The pill gave her migraines so birth control had been on him, and he'd been careless.

The color began to return to Zack's face. "I'm sorry."

"So am I."

"What are you going to do?"

"I don't know yet," Luke confessed. "There's been too much going on."

But he'd already discovered he wanted this baby. Even if he'd make a terrible father and the timing was wrong. The mother was, too. The night in the studio with Mara, when he'd forgotten the condom... If only that had been his careless mistake.

Zack switched into practical accountant mode. It had been a source of great amusement to their parents that Zack, who came across as so irresponsible, was actually the son with the most common sense.

"Don't marry her," he said.

"I haven't thought that far ahead." It had crossed Luke's mind, though. He had to get past this noose Denise had around his neck and focus on what was best for the baby.

"I mean it," Zack insisted. "A... friend married a man

because she was pregnant and it turned into a nightmare for her. For her daughter, too."

So that was Posey's story. A few weeks ago he would have told Zack to keep his nose out of her problems, but he had no right to talk. At least things were going reasonably well for Jake and Lacey—if only Jake would learn to make time for her every once in a while.

"I'd like to think I wouldn't be somebody's nightmare," Luke said.

"Denise will be yours." Zack studied his face. A frown shadowed his brow. "Especially if she finds out about Mara. Who is gorgeous, by the way." He drummed his fingers on the desk. "I can see why Dan McKillop has the hots for her."

A hot, serrated knife plunged deep in Luke's gut. Dan was the county sheriff and Ian McKillop's son. He liked women—and women liked him.

Luke suggested Dan do something physically impossible to himself.

"Don't marry Denise," Zack said again, as if Luke had just proved some point.

"And don't you say anything about this to Jake just yet. He's got enough to worry about." Luke picked up his glasses. "I've got a tutorial to run." At least computer science made sense. "Can you help Mac put Thunder in the paddock with the other horses when he's done with the lead rope?"

"Okay." Zack stood. "But you need to talk to Mara. Soon. Because I'm not going for Saturday morning coffee ever again. Those women are ruthless." His full-body shudder was only partly for effect. Luke got it. Married women couldn't stand to leave bachelors alone and the kids gave them a reason to pry. No parts of the brothers' lives were off-limits, anymore. "Finn's dance lessons are your problem, not mine."

Chapter Eleven

LUKE WAS ALONE in the family room, drinking a beer and watching the late news, ignoring the wreckage of toys and half-eaten crackers around him, when his phone rang. The kids were in bed. So were Jake and Zack.

Mara's number displayed. She'd never called him before.

No way could he answer. She'd ask why he hadn't called her like he'd promised, or showed up for Finn's classes, and he'd blurt out the truth.

He wasn't delivering his news over the phone. He'd send her a text in the morning saying he hadn't had time to call because he'd been too busy helping Jake. He'd say he was asleep when she called—none of which stretched credibility. Life on the ranch was hectic and he should be sleeping.

But no way could he answer. If he did, he'd tell her everything—and then he'd never see her again.

He snatched up the phone before it could go to voice mail.

"I'm coming over," he said, hanging up on her before she could utter a word.

He dumped his half-finished beer down the kitchen sink, grabbed his keys from the hook by the door, and fifteen minutes later, let himself into the darkened studio. He flipped one of the light switches—the one for the gray metallic fixture over the stairs. Its glow extended far enough to catch the first mirrors, which then reflected soft rays of light to the far end of the room. A limp white towel hung over one of the barres. She'd been working out.

He recalled in vivid detail the last workout he'd shared with her on that very same barre. Pain lanced through his chest.

He grabbed the stair railings, taking the steps two at a time. The shaky aluminum contraption swayed under his weight. He should have replaced it with something safer for her weeks ago.

She'd heard him arrive and was waiting for him by the door. Her dark hair was pinned in a tight ballerina bun that made the contrast between her crystal blue eyes and light olive skin that much more plain. A thin pink tank top announced she wasn't wearing a bra. Short, pale-gray boxers topped off long legs and bare, calloused feet.

He loved the way she wrapped those legs around him while he was sheathed deep inside her. He loved the soft sounds of pleasure she made as he moved. He especially loved holding her in his arms afterward, while they talked. When they were in bed together, nothing mattered but her.

His throat felt tight and scratchy. Normally, when he arrived, she threw herself into his arms. Instead, she kept a few feet of distance between them that felt more like a mile. She was never going to want to see him again after tonight, but he had to do what was right. He didn't know how to start.

She didn't have the same problem. Hot, Latina temper showed in her blue eyes as she studied him. "Why tell me you were going out of town on business? Why not simply say you were going to Seattle?"

He could hardly explain that he'd wanted to ease his conscience regarding Denise when he'd just finished reassuring her that their relationship was over.

"I was going to kill two birds with one stone. Denise kept insisting we needed to talk and I was going to tell her about you and let her know I'd moved on. I also wanted to pack up my apartment and give my notice at the college. My life is here, with my family."

And now he was going to have family in Seattle, too.

The hurt in Mara's eyes cut him. She knew there was more to the story. "But you didn't tell her about me."

"I did."

"What did she say?"

Luke drew a deep breath. There was no point in holding back. He wanted to tell her. He wanted to talk about it. He wanted her to reassure him that things would work out between them, even though he didn't see how they could. He was so damned tired of loss.

"She said she's pregnant."

The color drained from Mara's face. She clutched the edge of the kitchen island to brace herself. Luke took a step toward her, concern for her overriding everything else, but she held up a hand to keep him away. "Don't touch me."

Those three words stung worse than if she'd slapped him.

The minutes crawled by. He stared at the wall, giving her as much privacy as he dared to fully absorb his announcement. If she'd been even half as shocked as he was, then this had to be rough.

"What are you going to do?" she finally asked.

"I don't know," he said, which wasn't true. He knew what he had to do—it just wasn't what he wanted. He'd have a few months to come to terms with it all, because he'd stay in Grand as long as he could. Denise being pregnant didn't change the fact that his brothers and the kids needed him, too. "I had all kinds of plans for you and me. I was going to show you around the ranch. I thought you might like to learn how to ride—that is, if you don't ride already," he added, pausing when he realized he had no idea whether she could or not.

There were so many things he didn't know about her. He wanted to learn them all.

"I don't," she said.

"They perform the Nutcracker at the Billings Symphony over Christmas. I planned to take you," he continued, hanging on to the dream because she was listening to him. Maybe she shouldn't. He was telling her things that no longer mattered.

A flash of what looked like pain crossed her face. "And now you can't, because you'll be in Seattle with your wife and new baby."

"I didn't say that."

"But that's what's going to happen. You and Denise..." Mara stumbled a bit over the name, then gamely carried on.

"You were engaged. You haven't been split up for very long. You've got to still have feelings for her, and she clearly has feelings for you. Plus, you have common interests. You're both going to do what's best for the baby and I can understand that."

Mara was right, but she was wrong, too. All of Luke's frustration at a situation beyond his control boiled over. "Why would marrying her be best for the baby when I know that sooner or later, we'd end up dragging the poor kid through a divorce?"

He heard what he'd said. *Sonofabitch.* Zack was right. He couldn't marry Denise. Relief eased the tight pain that had tied his insides in knots for days. That was one choice now off the table.

But what else was he supposed to do?

Another option struck him and he seized it. "Come with me to Seattle."

It would be perfect. Mara could teach dance there as well as here.

She looked at him as if he'd lost his mind. "So I can rub the fact that I'm sleeping with you while she's pregnant with your child in her face? Can you imagine how much she must hate me right now?"

And she accused him of overthinking. "You have nothing to do with any of this."

Mara threw up her hands. "Of course I do. You ended a relationship with her while you were hurting over what happened to your parents and sister. You started one with me while you were angry with her—against your better judgment, I might add. I was the one who told you we could do this. That we shouldn't worry about the future. That we could keep things casual between us. And look at us. If I hadn't wanted you so badly, if I hadn't interfered, then you'd be with her right now."

She wanted him. Hearing her say it with such absolute certainty had his heart pounding, even though a sense of impending doom overrode any thrill.

He edged closer. He wasn't letting her walk away from him. "But I'm not with her. I'm with you. This is where I want to be."

"You don't know what you want," Mara said. "You've had too much happen for you to think clearly. It's been less than three months since you lost your family, you've ended an engagement, and you began an affair that was supposed to mean nothing. You gave up your career. And now you're going to be a father. Maybe I was wrong. Maybe you should think about the future. Where do you see yourself in your child's life? How big a part do you plan to play?"

That drew him up short. The thought of a child—*his* child—growing up without his active involvement hit too close to home. His sister Liz would never see the milestones in her kids' lives. Lydia would start school without her mother to see her off. She and the boys would graduate, go to college, get married, and have children of their own. His parents, too, would never know their upcoming grandchild. His son or daughter would never know their grandparents, either.

He'd play a part in his child's life. But why did he have

to do it without Mara?

"I know one thing I want," he said. "I want you. I *need* you. Don't push me away."

"I'm not." Mara's beautiful face softened. The temper in her eyes had long since disappeared, replaced by a wistful regret that he didn't like. "But I'm not going to influence your decisions anymore, Dr. Pretty. I've made things hard enough on you already. How you decide to deal with this is up to you. Until then, I don't think we should see each other." She held out her hand. Her fingers remained steady. Resolute eyes fastened on his. "I'd like my key back."

"No!" his brain shouted, even as he pulled the key from his pocket.

He clenched it in his fist, unwilling to let it go. He fixed the room in his head. The loft glowed with her presence. When he'd first seen the warehouse, and figured out that she lived here, he'd been appalled. But she'd turned the main level into a business, and the upstairs apartment into a home that was cozy and warm, and he'd felt as much at peace here with her as he did at the ranch. She made him happy in ways he couldn't begin to describe.

And yet, so far, not one thing he'd done for her had brought her the joy he longed to see on her face. She'd dealt with her own disappointments and setbacks alone. He had no business thrusting his problems on her.

The key scorched his skin as he transferred it from his palm to hers.

"You've made nothing hard on me. *Nothing*," he said.

His throat burned a little. If she thought she could tell

him she wanted him, and look at him with so much regret, then expect him to give her up, she had another thing coming. He cleared his throat. Telling her he needed her had been the wrong thing to say, because she'd misunderstood. He didn't need her help to make his decisions for him, or to do what was right. He needed her the way his lungs needed air.

He caught hold of her hand and pulled her in for a kiss. Just a quick one, because he agreed they both should step back and see where their futures were headed and if they could ever align.

"Don't give up on us," he added. "I won't be."

Leaving her was one of the hardest things he'd ever done. He sat in his car for a while, wrapped in darkness, facing the closed gate of the cemetery where his parents now rested. He wished he could ask them for advice.

They'd had such a happy marriage. They'd loved him and his brothers and sister, but there had also been a relationship between them that hadn't involved family. His mother had once said that her children would grow up and leave her, but her husband was with her forever.

When he pictured forever, he pictured Mara.

He planned to get that key back from her. This time, however, he intended to earn it.

"MARA, CAN YOU flip pancakes for a few minutes?" Diana asked.

Her cheeks were red from the heat. Strands of hair stuck to her forehead and neck. She was still breastfeeding and Randy was giving her a hand signal from one of the picnic tables that said the baby was hungry and refused to be pacified by anything else.

Mara moved into position on the assembly line, taking the spatula from her friend's hand and guarding the golden pancakes sizzling on one of the six electric griddles hooked up to a string of industrial-sized extension cords. The cords led to a power supply at one of the local businesses close by.

Grand celebrated Founder's Day on the second of August each year. Rain had finally broken the drought and the past few days had seen spattering remnants of the deluge, but today had dawned clear. A giant tent had been set up on the Yellowstone's riverfront boardwalk, where the local ladies' auxiliary annual breakfast had begun at seven that morning to kick-start events. It was now fast approaching nine o'clock and the crowd showed no signs of letting up.

Mara wished her knee could say the same, but she was having too much fun to bow out. Hay sculptures were to be judged at ten, while barrel racing and team roping events began at eleven. There'd be a picnic lunch and face painting for the children.

She'd been asked to enter one of her classes in the talent show scheduled for later that afternoon. While it was tempting to choose the youngest children because of the cuteness appeal, she'd opted for the fifteen-year-olds. They were less likely to bolt and run when they performed in front of a crowd. They also illustrated her teaching abilities the best.

After the talent show came the barbecue, then a parade, and finally, a street dance. A large section of Yellowstone Drive running through the downtown would be cordoned off. The night would end with a fireworks display.

She'd seen Luke the past few Saturday mornings since he'd broken his news because he'd had to bring Finn to class. He'd stopped calling her because she didn't answer, but she'd read his texts, and those came every day. She'd responded to those. He could be pretty funny.

He'd asked her to save a dance for him, tonight. She hadn't responded to that.

She wasn't ready to give up on him, but she'd meant it when she said she'd influenced him enough. A real relationship was about a lot more than sex, no matter how great the sex was. Diana and Randy were a shining example, as were her own parents, and while she and Luke might have been on the cusp of something more, they hadn't progressed beyond being lovers.

He was going to be a father. Any decisions he made from now on would have to be with that in mind. And she'd have to accept them, no matter how painful it was. She'd recover.

She removed the pancakes from the griddle and slid them onto a waiting plate.

"Hi, Mara."

She looked up. "Hi, Dan."

She smiled at the rugged blond sheriff. He was her landlord's grandson and she'd gone out with him a few times. She liked him but there'd been something missing.

Dan ignored the long lineup forming behind him. "Will

you be at the dance tonight?"

She wasn't sure if she should. Luke planned to be there, and if he tried to claim that dance he'd asked her to save, she wouldn't say no. She missed him. She missed the intimacy. She missed their talks the most, which surprised her, considering how little they had in common.

"I'm thinking about it," she said.

"Why don't I swing by and give you a lift?"

"Thank you," she said, "but it's only a few minutes' walk from the studio. I can manage."

Dan was another overprotective cowboy who'd tried to coddle her because of her damaged leg, and she didn't want that. Her knee was getting stronger every day. Standing around serving pancakes was harder than walking, and yet, here she was.

"See you tonight, then." Dan moved on toward the supply of sausage and bacon keeping warm under the heat lamp at the end of the line.

The crowd had begun to thin out. Mara looked around. Cars were lined along Yellowstone Drive for as far as the eye could see. The parking lot butting the boardwalk was packed. A few spaces had opened up, however, as the early risers who'd shown up mainly for the food began to depart. A familiar car occupied one of the vacated spaces.

That was all she had time to note. The pancake line began moving again.

"I'm back," Diana announced. She nudged Mara aside with her hip. "Go get your breakfast. You've been standing long enough."

Mara filled her plate with a stack of pancakes and found a spot at one of the picnic tables. She set her plate down and went to get a cup of coffee. When she returned, Luke was getting the children settled into the empty seats next to hers. He glanced at her and her breath caught. Now she knew what was missing with Dan. He wasn't Luke.

Four pairs of black-lashed, striking green eyes assailed her.

"Finn asked if we could sit with you," Luke said. "I hope you don't mind."

"Not at all." What else could she say?

Who could resist four pairs of McGregor eyes?

"Hi, Miss Ramos." Finn wriggled on the bench, his energy level approaching full throttle. She bit the inside of her lip. Someone was going to sleep well tonight. "Uncle Luke says I can ride a sheep."

"They have a sheep rodeo for the little kids," Mac, who was a more mature ten, supplied. His tone strongly inferred he wouldn't be caught dead participating. "I'm going to train my horse for team roping."

Luke passed Lydia to Mac. "Keep an eye on your sister while I get the pancakes."

Mara's phone chirped a few minutes later. She retrieved her phone from her jeans pocket and read the text. "*I hear Dan McKillop has herpes.*"

She smiled. Another text flashed. "*Herpes is no laughing matter.*"

"What's so funny?" Finn asked.

"Mind your own business," Mac told him.

Mara felt a small hand on her leg. She peered under the table. A sweet little face peered back.

"Up," Lydia said. She tried to stand and bumped her blond, fluff-tufted head. "Ow." Tears flooded enormous green eyes and she started to cry.

Mac half stood, preparing to launch himself across the table and rescue his sister, proving the protective gene ran deep in the McGregor clan. For some of them, at least. Finn took a look, decided Lydia would live, and went back to business as usual.

"I've got her," Mara reassured Mac. She reached down with both hands, took the little girl under the arms, and carefully maneuvered her onto her knee. "Let me see where it hurts, honey." She examined the bump. "All it needs is a kiss." She pressed her lips to the fuzzy mop, breathing deep. Lydia smelled like baby and bubblegum shampoo, two irresistible scents.

Lydia settled her padded bottom on Mara's lap, making herself at home, the bump forgotten as she spotted the cooling pancakes on Mara's plate. Mara cut off a small morsel, dipped it in maple syrup, and popped it in Lydia's mouth. Lydia chewed, swallowed, and opened her mouth for more.

"Uncle Jake says Lyddie eats like a horse," Finn said.

Shame on Uncle Jake.

"There's nothing wrong with a growing girl owning a healthy appetite," Mara replied.

She was curious about Mac. She already knew Finn and Lydia. He looked a lot like Luke, but as if smiling might hurt him. He watched his younger siblings like a hawk—or maybe a mother hen. Her heart went out. Luke said he was taking the loss of his parents the hardest, and had a few anger issues, but that Jake had it well in hand.

"Tell me about your horse," Mara said to him. "Why do you want to teach it to be a team roper?"

Mac's grim expression lightened a notch. "Uncle Jake knows all about horses and team roping and he said he'll help."

By the time Luke returned with four plates, two empty and two of them heavily loaded with food, she'd heard all about Thunder and how amazing he was. It was also plain that Mac idolized Jake, the uncle Mara hadn't yet met.

Luke set the plates down and began dividing the food. Once the children were eating, he made a few extra trips for coffee and juice.

He sat down next to Mac, across from Mara. He smiled at her. Brown hair, almost black, flopped over his forehead into his eyes and he flipped it back with his fingers.

"Are we having fun yet?" he asked.

"I can't speak for others, but I am," she replied, holding the tiny plastic cup filled with apple juice for Lydia to sip from.

She was. She liked children, and these three were well-mannered and sweet. She had Lydia on her lap and Finn snuggled up as close as he could get without ousting his sister. Mac had lost a lot of his sullen air, excited about the rodeo events he'd get to see for the first time. It seemed "cowboy" was genetic. Montana was going to be good for him.

And Luke…

He was going to make a fantastic father.

She'd been so angry at first, when she thought he'd had his fun and lost interest in her, forgetting how complicated his circumstances were. It hadn't once occurred to her that those circumstances might have become more complicated still.

Ignoring reality was her issue to overcome. From the beginning, he'd tried his best to be realistic and she'd convinced him to set responsibility aside. She didn't begrudge him his pending fatherhood, but she'd visited the orphanage where her mother volunteered. She'd witnessed how starved for adult affection those children were. Lydia and Finn, both so eager for a woman's attention, were another shining example of children in need.

She refused to compete with a child.

Luke reached for his phone, casually flicking the buttons. Her phone, sitting on the weathered wooden table beside her, chirped again.

"*Me too. Save me that dance.*"

Chapter Twelve

A FTER THE BARBECUE, Mara went home to shower and change.

The girls' talent show performance that afternoon had gone off without a hitch. They'd teamed up with their high school show choir, chosen a jazz number from the movie *Chicago* to perform, and it had been fun. A little scandalous for Grand Town Day, perhaps. But Mara had dialed the dance routine back to PG and she was so proud of them. Even better, they were proud of themselves.

Days like today reminded her of why she liked teaching.

She chose a short dress, a deep, purple eggplant in color, with a rounded tunic hemline that came to mid-thigh. The off-the-shoulder neckline attached to long sleeves that flared wide at the cuffs. She added dramatic eye makeup and a dark lipstick that matched her dress, and left her hair loose. Delicate gold bangles and enormous hooped earrings dragged the eye upward, away from her knee. After waffling back and forth over the best shoes for the dress, she settled on ballet flats better suited for dancing.

She'd considered skipping the dance tonight altogether. Then, she'd asked herself why. Because she didn't think she'd enjoy it?

Or because there was only one man she wanted to dance with and she hadn't yet made up her mind?

Luke hadn't lingered after finishing breakfast. He'd brought the children for their entertainment, not his, and that one final text was the last she'd received from him all day, to her disappointment. His texts never failed to make her smile.

She was getting a stronger sense of the man he'd been before disaster befell him, and he was proving a hard man to resist. Worse, she was finding out what she stood to lose. It terrified her because she knew in her heart that his ex-fiancée, the mother of his child, wasn't going to give up on him without a fight, and in the end, Luke would do what he believed to be right. He had to be able to live with himself.

Why would he give up so much for a woman he'd only known a few months?

The walk from her studio to the waterfront didn't take long. She carried a cane that she used when her leg was tired, and after a long day, yes, she was unsteady, and therefore, not taking chances. Falling in front of Luke had been humiliating enough, although she'd gotten over it almost at once. He hadn't turned it into a big deal.

If she fell in front of the whole town, however, she'd have to move.

Clouds blackened the sky, hiding the moon, but the meteor shower lights crisscrossed from poles along the length of the boardwalk picked up the slack. The band had set up under the tent and they were conducting a sound check on their gear. A speaker squawked. Beyond the boardwalk, the slow, lazy waters of the Yellowstone River swirled past. The drought that had plagued Grand all summer had finally ended, but while it had spit drizzle a few times off and on throughout the day, the night remained calm and mild. The picnic tables had been pushed back to line the river's edge. Bales of hay had been brought in for people to sit on.

She looked around for familiar faces and saw Lacey Anderson, sitting with a few of the soccer moms, who also happened to be dance moms. Grand really was small.

She liked the town. More than any other place she'd lived in her life. Its size was part of the appeal. She'd been made to feel welcome here at a point in her life when she'd needed people behind her who were more intent on protecting her right to privacy than in defending her reputation. Her family might be amazing, and they loved her, but they didn't understand the American culture at all.

Mara joined the women. She squeezed in beside Lacey, who gave off a satisfied air, as if all was right in her world. Mara was happy for her. Lacey was a good friend.

"How's your brother?" she asked, then wished she hadn't, because Lacey's cheerful smile dimmed.

"Still not speaking to family."

"I'm sorry."

Lacey's contentment had nothing to do with her brother, then. That left only one likely option. She must have Jake McGregor right where she wanted him—which didn't explain why she was here by herself. Maybe it was Jake's night to look after the children, but if so, why wasn't Lacey with him, helping out?

If Jake was anything like Luke, Mara could guess. He would never introduce a woman into his young niece and nephews' lives until he was sure she'd be permanent.

"No need to be sorry," Lacey said, recovering her smile. "It's by Clayton's own choice, and if that's what he wants, then there's nothing more I can do."

She was right. People made their own choices.

Mara tucked her cane behind one of the bales of hay as the mostly Southern rock band kicked off with a popular hit by Little Big Town. A few of the husbands drifted over to claim their wives for a dance and the boardwalk began filling with people. Someone urged Lacey to her feet.

Mara's toe tapped. Hay scratched the backs of her thighs. She longed to get up and join them. Her scarred leg, that people politely pretended not to notice, made it highly unlikely anyone—anyone but Luke—would ask.

Dan McKillop sat down beside her. "Hey," he said, bumping her shoulder. "Thought I'd come keep you company for a bit."

Mara didn't want company. She wanted to *dance*.

"Seriously, McKillop?" a familiar voice drawled from behind them, the sound drifting over her head. "You're keeping a dance instructor company at a dance by sitting with her?"

Mara looked around. Her heart sprang to life. Even though she'd known he would be here, she couldn't help the twitch of excitement the sight of him gave her.

Luke stepped over the row of baled hay and onto the

boardwalk, looking exactly like what he was—a scholarly rancher. He wore a cowboy hat, hipster jeans, and white canvas shoes, with unabashed ease. Somehow, it worked.

He extended a hand. "Shall we show the sheriff how it's done?"

She didn't think twice. She did want to dance and she trusted Luke more than anyone else to keep her from falling. She wasn't sure everyone in Grand would be onboard with his methods, however, if the mixed reactions to the dance routine that afternoon were any basis for judgment.

At least they had their clothes on.

The band shifted into a waltz by the Nitty Gritty Dirt Band. Luke placed a hand on the small of her back, pressing her against him, and turned her ever so slightly so that her weak leg was braced by his hip, thigh, and knee on that side. They were close, possibly indecently so, yet not indecent enough to incite more than a ripple of gossip.

He bent his head.

"You can let me lead," he whispered into her ear, his voice low, reassuring, and above all, so tantalizing. "This is the kind of dancing I know."

After a few steps, she relaxed in his arms. He really did.

"Didn't I warn you about herpes?" he chastised her.

He was jealous. It shouldn't make her feel so good, but it did. "I had no idea you could catch herpes by dancing, Dr. Pretty."

"See? Right there is the reason why my PhD comes in so handy. You'd never know these things if I didn't verify them for you," he replied. "I can sort fact from fiction online."

She laughed, then lost herself to the music. She'd danced with a lot of men, the majority of them professionals, and yet dancing with Luke, and having to trust him so completely, was a different experience entirely. He knew every inch of her body. He caught every falter before it occurred.

The song ended too soon. He'd maneuvered her to the far edge of the crowd, close to, but not quite into, the shadows beyond the sparkling shower of overhead lights. A fine spattering of raindrops speckled her bare shoulders, cooling her skin.

"Let me take you home tonight," Luke said, carefully keeping his voice low so their neighbors couldn't hear.

The request brought her back to earth. Nothing was settled.

Another song struck up, this one by Lynyrd Skynyrd.

"I don't think so," Mara said. "It's—"

Dan tapped Luke on the shoulder. "Thanks for showing me how it's done," he said, a spark of humor warming his eyes. "Mind if I cut in?"

Luke's face was too easy to read. He was frustrated by the interruption, and about to say yes, he did mind, and Mara didn't want him starting something he might later regret. Dan wasn't competition, and deep down, Luke knew it. Also, if she recalled correctly, Dan and Zack McGregor were good friends.

But maybe avoiding Luke wasn't the right approach to be taking. He was a private man who rarely discussed what was troubling him, and not unlike Finn, he had a lot of pent-up, pressure-cooker emotions that required a release. She'd offered him no-strings-attached, casual sex, which had taken the edge off, but that had blown up in their faces because it was difficult for either one of them to make smart choices when sex clouded their reasoning.

She had a much better idea.

"I'd love to dance," she said to Dan. She touched Luke's arm as she brushed past him. "I'll talk to you later."

IT WAS THE Saturday morning after the dance.

A burst of rain had ended Grand's summer drought and the grass had bounced back, thick and healthy. The prime market for hay was for horses and the drought had driven the prices sky high. The Wagging Tongue Ranch had to make the cut, let it dry for a day or so in the heat, and then bale it, all while the weather was good.

Because Mac had soccer practice which Jake refused to miss, Luke and Zack had drawn tractor duty. Luke was cutting today. Zack was running the baler in one of the fields that had already been cut.

Since Luke couldn't take Finn to dance class, he'd resorted to bribery. At five, Finn rarely got to ride on the tractors and he'd thrown dance over without hesitation. Luke lifted him into the cab of the tractor and buckled him in. He loaded a blanket and a cooler filled with snacks next.

Luke loved the new tractor. The ranch had bought it in the spring before his dad passed away. It had air conditioning, an extra seat for small passengers, and best of all, an automatic tracking guidance system that allowed him to plot how the fields should be cut. The trick would be to keep Finn's little fingers off the touch screen.

He'd stowed the .338 Winchester Magnum rifle behind the driver's seat. The bear Jake had been hunting was still on the loose and the ranches in the area had been losing too many cattle. Trying to capture and relocate it would simply make it somebody else's problem, so the ranch hands had been ordered to shoot it on sight.

Luke started the engine and maneuvered the tractor out of the yard. Finn chattered away beside him, requiring nothing more than the occasional acknowledgement that Luke was listening—which he wasn't—allowing Luke's thoughts to wander.

He was still out of sorts over the dance. Not angry, exactly, because he had no reason to be, and not necessarily jealous, because he had no real right, but definitely not in his happy place. Mara wouldn't let him take her home. Then, watching Dan do his best to help her dance, and worse, succeeding, had inspired all sorts of resentment, so he'd chosen to leave rather than end up making a fool out of himself and embarrassing her.

But she hadn't called or texted so they could talk, as she'd promised. He didn't know what to make of that, or what he should do about it.

And then there was Denise. He'd called every day, trying to find out how she was feeling and when her next doctor's appointment was, and if she'd like him to be there for it—this was his baby, too—but as soon as he'd said he couldn't stay because work on the ranch wouldn't wait, she'd shut him out, too.

Women. Right now his PhD was worth crap.

He shifted the tractor's gears with a bit too much force.

His route took him toward Camelback Butte and the Badlands. An irrigation system cut through the Wagging Tongue Ranch and ran toward craggy hills dotted with ponderosa, and the butte beyond, but the irrigation feeding off the Tongue River was intended for watering the livestock. The ranch practiced crop rotation with its fields, allowing them to lie fallow for a season. Cattle grazed on that land.

The range, with plenty of low, rolling hills, wasn't flat, but visibility was good and Luke could see for miles. The size of the wake of turkey vultures far off in the distance, their enormous wings flapping as they skipped around whatever carcass they fed on, tipped him off that the ranch had another cow down. Whether or not the bear was the reason remained to be seen.

He considered investigating. He had Finn with him, however, and Finn, who didn't have an understanding of death, had just lost his parents and grandparents, so Luke decided against it. The vultures would be picking the carcass clean and it wasn't the nicest sight.

He'd let Jake know about it, instead.

A lone rider cut out from behind a stand of juniper that crested a knoll, headed on an intersection course with the tractor. Luke sighed when he saw who it was. He cut the engine and rolled down the window on the cab door.

"You boys are hard to pin down," Weldon Scott remarked.

Dust flecked the hat shading his eyes. His horse's ears flicked a few times and its tail swished. Something had made it nervous. Probably a bear. The butt of a rifle jutted out of the scabbard attached to his saddle. Jake said Weldon had been hunting it, too.

"It's a busy time of year," Luke replied.

Finn, naturally inquisitive, craned his neck, anxious to be part of the conversation. "Hi."

Weldon grinned at him. "Well, well. Hello. If it isn't little Fun."

"Finn," the boy corrected him.

"Really?" Weldon pretended surprise. "I could have sworn someone told me you were Fun."

"I am," Finn said.

"It's nice to meet you, Fun."

Finn, who was smart, caught on that he was being teased and made a face, but it was obvious that he enjoyed it. Which, Luke decided, earned Weldon a hearing. Having grandchildren had mellowed the old man.

"I'd like to get together and talk business someday real soon," Weldon said, getting straight to the point Luke was expecting. "I have a proposition for you."

"You should talk to Jake, then. The business is his."

Luke had given up on the dream of keeping his share of the ranch the instant he'd learned he was about to become a father. He'd be moving back to Seattle in February for good. He had no other choice. Until then, he'd fly back once a month to check on Denise and give her what support he could—both financial and moral. He'd prove he could step up.

Obstinateness stitched Weldon's gray brows into a single straight seam across his forehead under the brim of his hat. "I want to talk to all three of you."

Luke could be stubborn, too. "Sorry, Weldon. You'll have to arrange it with Jake."

"You boys are so much like your father." The older man sighed. "There was no reasoning with him either."

The dig at his father crossed a line and Luke couldn't take it. He started the engine and Weldon's horse backed away a few steps.

"Happy hunting," he said.

Luke cut hay for a few hours, the tractor bouncing over the ground, until Finn became too restless to sit still. It was time for a break. He stopped the tractor, turned off the engine, and settled Finn on the blanket in the tractor's shade with the cooler of sandwiches. He dug out a juice box for Finn and a cold bottle of cola for himself.

"What's this?" Finn asked, plucking a small plant and holding it out for Luke's inspection. It had a long head with pink-tipped lobes instead of petals.

"Clover," Luke said, although what kind, he couldn't say.

"And this?"

It had a blue, multi-headed blossom and a long stem. Luke searched his memory. His mother had loved field flowers. So had Liz. "Triteleia, I think."

Finn tucked it into his pocket. "I'm going to save it for

Mommy."

"Uh…" Luke said, not sure where to begin. "Your mom would love that you'd do that for her, but she can't come back to get it, so you might want to give it to Posey, instead."

"She can too come back." Finn sounded pretty definite about it. "I heard her talking to Uncle Jake."

"You must have been dreaming," Luke said, as gently as possible. This was so hard.

"No, I wasn't. She was out on the front doorstep one night with Uncle Jake," Finn insisted. "I heard her. But she thought I was sleeping so she didn't come tuck me in."

Lacey must be visiting Jake when Luke and Zack were out, after the kids were in bed.

On the one hand, Luke was relieved. He'd worried Jake might completely blow things with her, especially after he'd seen her at the Town Days dance, alone. On the other hand, however, it wasn't good for Finn to keep these fantasies alive in his head. Luke was about to explain to Finn that he'd heard someone else when a movement in the distance caught his attention.

A large black blob was headed toward them, approaching at a faster clip than Luke liked. Seconds later, he could tell what it was—although he'd already known. The bear must have been hanging close to its kill and smelled the sandwiches in their picnic cooler.

"Get in the cab," Luke said to Finn, scooping his nephew up by the underarms and dumping him in the tractor. "Stay right there, bud. Don't you dare move."

He slammed the door shut and jogged around to the driver's side. He grabbed the rifle from behind the seat and the ammunition from under it, then loaded the rifle as fast as he could. He checked on Finn. He had his face pressed to the door of the cab but showed no signs of attempting to get out.

The bear, enormous, barreled toward Luke at full speed. Damn, it was fast. It had smelled humans in its territory for long enough now that it no longer had any fear. Luke braced the rifle against his shoulder and his feet firm on the ground, prepared for the kickback. He'd loaded a high-caliber bullet and it packed quite a wallop.

He was a good shot and he aimed for the lungs. The first bullet caught the bear high on the shoulder, stopping its forward projection, but only for a few seconds. The wound would enrage it. Besides, Luke couldn't allow it to live. It had been killing cattle.

He chambered another bullet and walked toward it, keeping his sight on its chest, searching for the right angle to shoot for the heart. The bear snorted, rolled, and scrambled to its feet, then reared on its hind legs. Luke squeezed the trigger. The recoil snapped his shoulder back, which brought the barrel of the rifle up, but he'd compensated for that. The bear dropped to the ground, motionless.

Luke's ears rang a little. He waited to make sure the bear wasn't planning to move. He couldn't bring himself to put another bullet into the animal as a guarantee.

Instead, he checked to make sure Finn was where he had left him, which he was, then he set the rifle on the ground at his feet so he could grab it fast if he had to, and took out his phone. He'd need a few more people to bring a wagon to help get the bear carcass back to the ranch. He couldn't lift that much dead weight by himself.

Sound gradually returned as he scrolled through his contacts, searching for one of the teenaged ranch hands. The shots had spooked a ring-necked pheasant. It flopped around, faking an injury while it decided the level of danger Luke posed for its harem, then scurried into the long grass and disappeared.

Luke picked up the rifle, still uneasy about turning his back on the animal even though that shot to the heart would have been instantly fatal, but Finn was a bigger concern now.

The boy, wide-eyed and excited, the sun catching the red of his hair when he bent his head, reached to open the door of the cab when he saw his uncle walking toward him. He caught the stern warning on Luke's face, however, and wisely withdrew his hand.

Luke stowed the rifle behind the seat and put the ammunition away, taking his time so he could think about what to do and say next. He wished Jake were here, because Luke was going to have to finish that chat with Finn about death, and Jake was so much better at it.

He opened the door and lifted Finn to the ground.

"Can I touch it?" Finn shouted, his eyes on the bear. The kid was so overcharged that his whole body quivered.

Luke's adrenaline hadn't yet worn off, either. There was nothing like facing down a charging bear while he had an unpredictable, excitable little boy out of his line of vision to drive home the meaning of danger.

"Not until Devon and Pete get here with the wagon," he said. "While we're waiting, you and I need to talk about what being dead means."

Then he was going to have a talk with Mara about the meaning of life and how it could be snatched away in an instant. Maybe about what she meant to him, too. And he was doing it in person. The day he'd met her had been the luckiest of his life, despite the unfortunate circumstances that brought him back to Montana. He wasn't giving up on her.

She didn't get to give up on him, either.

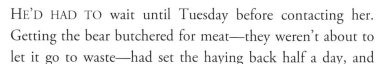

HE'D HAD TO wait until Tuesday before contacting her. Getting the bear butchered for meat—they weren't about to let it go to waste—had set the haying back half a day, and he'd been on a tractor for sixteen hours straight, three days in a row.

Rather than exhausted, however, which was what he should be, right now he was antsy as hell. Before heading out, he'd sent her a text. "*It's later. I'll be there in an hour.*"

She'd texted him back. "*Wear something you don't mind getting dirty, Dr. Pretty.*"

What was that supposed to mean?

He was about to find out. He punched the doorbell, again regretting the loss of his key.

She had her purse over her shoulder and her car keys in her hand when she came to the door. A pink, stretchy halter top fastened around her neck by a narrow band of fabric. It bared her belly and shoulders, and the way it hugged her breasts made his fingers itch. The color really was better suited to girls—at least, from what he'd seen to date—so Jake was getting a pass for Lyddie's pink walls. Tight jeans molded her hips and she had sneakers on. He'd never seen her wear those, before. Her go-tos for footwear tended to be sandals and ballet flats.

"Going somewhere?" he inquired, then belatedly, re-membered how she'd schooled him about proper greetings. "I mean, hello. You look beautiful." He'd been so anxious to see her that he'd forgotten flowers completely. The ranch had a whole garden filled with blossoms gradually going to waste and he'd meant to pick some for her.

"Thank you," Mara replied. "And yes, I am going some-where. So are you."

Disappointment stung his heart. She wasn't letting him into her space. He knew how protective she was of it, and it seemed she now viewed him as a threat.

"I was hoping we could talk here. Just talk," he added hastily, in case she thought he'd expect something more.

"We can talk later."

He followed her down the cracked walk, across the street to the parking lot, and to her car. Her long ponytail held steady between her shoulders above the mesmerizing, elegant, dancer sway of her hips.

"We can take my car," he offered. "I'll drive."

"Or, we can take mine and I'll drive." She pushed the button on her key fob and popped the locks on her vehicle.

"Get in, Dr. Pretty."

"Yes, ma'am." He'd do whatever she wanted. Whatever it took.

He crammed into the passenger side, sliding the seat back to accommodate his long legs. The last passenger she'd had in her car must have been either a child or a woman—which didn't mean a damn thing, other than to put him more at ease. "Where are we going?"

"You'll see."

They didn't go far. Just before they hit the highway heading out of Grand, she turned down a side street. At the end of the street, on a corner, was a six-unit, one-level strip mall. She selected a parking spot in front of the business at the farthest end of the strip.

"The *Rage* Room?" Luke asked, quirking a brow in suspicion. What was this all about? What message was she trying to send?

Mara shouldered her door open and swung her legs out. She cast a look back, a bright spark of challenge in her blue eyes.

"Come on, Dr. Pretty," she said. "Let's see what you've got." She smiled at him, stealing his breath. "And if you've got more than I do."

Chapter Thirteen

THE RAGE ROOM was owned by one of Mara's dance mothers. Her clients were mostly women, or so she'd claimed when they'd commiserated over the pitfalls of small business ownership, so a last-minute, Tuesday night booking hadn't been a problem for her.

Luke pried himself out of the car, unfurling his body until he returned to full height. He rested his forearms on the car's roof. She stared at his hands. They'd lost their desk-job, pristine smoothness, instead displaying callouses and slight staining around the nail beds. Biceps bulged under the rolled cuffs of his denim shirt sleeves. He retained the overall look of a professor, but in the way a Rottweiler resembled a Doberman. He was no longer anything close to pretty, she suddenly realized. Luke had gone native.

Or, rather, he'd returned to his roots. Grand was where he belonged. Going back to Seattle would chip away at his soul. He'd never be happy there, something he'd already figured out.

But being away from his child would destroy him. He'd go back to his old life when the baby was born, and even if it broke her heart, Mara wouldn't stand in his way.

"You think I have anger issues?" He sounded more intrigued, possibly amused, than offended by any assumptions she'd made.

"I think we both might have them," she replied. "Let's go."

The inside of the Rage Room looked more like the entrance to a maximum security facility than a night out for working mothers with high levels of social frustration. A round reception desk faced the main door. The floor was bare, polished concrete. The stark white walls of the lobby were filled with photos of people in padded white coveralls, carrying ball bats and sledgehammers, surrounded by post-apocalyptic levels of mass destruction.

If the dance mother was surprised to see Luke and Mara together, she didn't let on. She walked them through the rules, explaining how everything worked, and had them sign disclosures. They donned protective gear—coveralls, helmets, goggles, and chest padding.

The steel-walled, prison-like room they were shown to sported a blinding, bare, overhead light and an odd assortment of options for smashing. Several kegs stood on end on the floor. Stacks of dishes and glasses perched on shelves. An old desk housed an ancient computer monitor—the kind that took up half the desk—a tower, and a printer. A sledgehammer and two baseball bats occupied a corner.

"I feel stupid," Luke said, once their host had departed.

"Why—because rage rooms are mostly for women?" Mara asked, her hands on her hips.

His green eyes laughed at her from behind the goggles.

Paired with the white coveralls and padding, he looked as if he should be sanitizing crime scenes. "No. Because I didn't think of this, myself." He picked up the sledgehammer and hefted it as if testing its weight. "That monitor's mine."

He swung the sledgehammer over his shoulder as if he were Thor, bringing it down with precision. The monitor casing cracked but stayed together. The screen remained whole.

"You hit like a girl," Mara said, poking him with the tip of her bat. "Except not as hard."

"Ha, ha." Luke hefted the sledgehammer onto his shoulder. "That was a test run. I'm warming up. Why don't you take a shot, too? But not at the monitor," he added. "Find your own issues to work on."

Mara eyed an ugly ceramic cookie jar in the shape of a cow. She had no issues with either cookies or cows, but if she closed her eyes and used her imagination, it wouldn't matter. She placed the jar on one of the kegs, scrunched her eyelids tightly together, swung the bat, and bashed it as hard as she could. Shards of ceramic pelted the wall.

She opened her eyes and surveyed the damage. It was difficult to put any real strength into her swing because she couldn't rely on her knee, but she'd made a respectable effort.

"How did that feel?" Luke inquired.

"Satisfying," Mara admitted. She picked up a plate and hurled it left-handed against the dented steel of the wall, using it as a discus. Splintered pieces showered the floor. "That, even more so."

He replaced the cookie jar with a stoneware crock pot. Then, his fingers closed around hers on the bat. "Here. Let me help you with this one."

"You're missing the point. We're supposed to be working out our personal anger issues," she said, but she let him put his arms around her so he could help her swing anyway. The crock pot tumbled off the keg and broke into three chunks on the floor.

"You need this more than I do. I can go out in a field and swing a post maul any day of the week," he said, his cheek pressed to hers. "Why do you think ranchers are so mellow?"

She spoke without thinking. "It's going to be harder to find a field in Seattle."

His arms dropped away. She swiveled toward him, wary about how the snide reminder had been received. She hadn't brought him here to create stress. This was supposed to relieve it.

"Excuse me," he said.

He snatched a glass tumbler from a shelf and hurled it against the wall. Bright sparkles flew.

At least she now knew for certain how he felt about Seattle.

"Don't forget the computer," she said.

He seized the sledgehammer. Two minutes later, pieces of the former monitor littered the floor and the tower had been demolished.

He adjusted his goggles, admiring his handiwork. "Not bad for a girl." Then, he looked at her and delivered a sharp barb of his own. "When you hear that song on the radio—the one where you danced in the video with Little Zee—how does it make you feel?"

No one had ever put it right in front of her like that before. She never spoke about it. She'd spent a year trying not to think about it, either. A hot red sheen blurred her vision. A vein throbbed in her temple, making her head ache. She propped a coffee maker on a keg and gripped the bat in both hands.

"Stand back," she said.

After that, they both got down to business.

She'd booked the room for forty minutes. When their time was up, they were panting and sweaty. Her knee ached, but in a smug, self-satisfied way.

Luke flung the bat he'd been using aside. It hit the steel wall with a clang. He took off his goggles and tossed them on a shelf. "Can we talk, now?"

Mara surveyed the room. The carnage they'd caused was inspiring. "What's the point? You're going back to Seattle."

His silence confirmed it. Her satisfaction evaporated, along with the anger she'd expended, leaving her tired and aching and empty.

Then, he regained his voice. "I'm not moving back to Seattle for good until the baby is due. Marry me," he said, his gaze green and steady on her. "If you're still worried about how Denise will take it, then we can get married right away and she'll have until February to get used to it."

"My God," Mara said. She slid her goggles down, letting them hang from her neck. "I thought you were different."

His brilliant brain made the connection. He blinked. His jaw slackened. "Did you just compare me to *Little Zee*?"

It was lucky for him she'd already worked off a good deal of her rage. "No. You did that yourself. Whether or not you still love Denise, you should have more respect for her than this."

"I don't love Denise. I love you."

She believed him. He loved her. Telling him she loved him too, however, wasn't going to make things any easier for him. Or her, either. She'd come into his life at a bad time. She'd offered him an escape from reality, which was what he'd wanted and needed. Maybe she had, too.

Unfortunately, sometimes reality really did bite—and when it bit, it bit hard.

"I've been in Denise's position. I've had someone who claimed he cared about me suddenly decide he didn't, and abandon me when I needed him, all because I'd become a problem."

"She was the one who walked out on *me*," Luke said. He was furious. His face had gone hard. "This changes nothing. I'm going back for the baby, not her."

"Once the baby is born, you and Denise will be spending a lot of time together. I'd only be in the way. I'm not dropping everything I've worked for here in Grand"—where she'd finally begun to feel as if she belonged—"so I can head to Seattle, only to discover I've become another one of your problems." The thought of starting over again, with so much uncertainty involved, was too daunting. She only had so much strength.

He swallowed. His Adam's apple bobbed up and down. She'd gone too far. She could almost see the wheels in his head spinning. Then, the fierceness went out of his face.

"Is that what you're so afraid of? That I'll forget how important you are to me? I love you, Mara. I've loved you from the moment you called me out for saying I was fixing your door as a favor to Diana. You understand me, and you call me on bullshit, just like you're doing right now." He rubbed his forehead with the flat of his palm. "Asking you to marry me while everything is a mess was stupid of me, wasn't it?"

Her heart was pounding with hope and relief. He'd finally begun to see reason. "The stupidest. How does it feel to be the dumb one for a change?"

"Please don't give up on me," he said, his voice raspy and gruff. "I've never loved anyone the way I love you."

She wanted to tell him she loved him, too—she did, with all her heart—but she wasn't ready to make that much of a commitment. Not when he had the potential to hurt her. If she didn't say it out loud no one would ever know, and if he changed his mind after the baby was born, she'd at least be left with her pride.

"Go to Seattle. Be there for Denise and the baby. Then, once you see how your life is going to be after the baby is born, we can talk about the future. I'll be right here, waiting for you," she said.

"I can't ask that of you."

"You aren't asking me. I'm telling you."

Strong, warm, work-hardened arms enfolded her. Chest protectors formed an awkward barrier between them. He rested his cheek on the top of her head. "I don't deserve you."

"No," Mara said, keeping things as light as she could, smiling even though she felt more like crying. "You really don't."

But really, he did.

"It's only August. February is a long way off. What do we do until then?" he asked.

She hugged his waist hard, leaning against him. Something crunched under her shoe. The last weeks had been incredibly difficult for them both, and the next six months wouldn't be easy, but she'd missed him and he needed her. Until then, she'd take what she could get.

"Let's go back to my place and see what we can come up with," she said.

The door to the room opened. The owner stuck her head in.

"Time's up," she said cheerfully. Then, "Oh. Excuse me."

And the door hastily closed.

"Saturday morning coffee is going to be a lot more uncomfortable from now on," Luke said. "It was bad enough to begin with."

But he didn't sound too bothered by it.

THE LATE SUMMER afternoon was sunny and hot.

It had been three weeks since the Rage Room. Luke had

finally persuaded Mara to spend the day at the ranch with him so he could take her riding and show her around.

He also planned to properly introduce her to his family. Specifically, Jake.

He was going to marry her. They hadn't discussed it again—he'd learned his lesson—but unless she could convince him that she no longer wanted him, it was going to happen. He'd told his brothers so. They'd both looked at him as if he'd lost his mind, but for slightly different reasons. Zack knew about the baby. Jake knew he'd recently asked another woman to marry him.

"You're supposed to be the smart one," Jake had said, and left it at that. He and Lacey had finally brought their relationship into the open, so he wasn't as inclined to be his usual critical self where Luke was concerned. He hadn't said a word when he found out about Finn taking dance lessons, either.

Zack, on the other hand…

"Dumbass." He bounced the heel of his palm off Luke's forehead. "I get that Mara is hot, but you don't have to propose to a woman every time you get laid. Try thinking with your head for a change."

"How's Posey doing these days?" Luke inquired, and the conversation stagnated right there.

"We aren't going far," he said to Mara now. "We'll take a ride along the river."

He helped her into the saddle, and after that, she was fine. She sat a horse as if she'd been riding her whole life.

The Tongue River was well-known for sports fishing.

There was a spot not far from the road where the McGregors had fished and swam when they were kids. Luke remembered Liz and her skimpy-bikini-clad girlfriends ducking and splashing in the water as if it were yesterday.

So many memories.

"You love it here, don't you?" Mara asked, studying his face.

The warm golden tan she'd acquired over the summer made the clear, startling blue of her eyes that much more pronounced. Long, slender legs, encased in tight jeans and high boots, hugged the docile, ancient roan he'd chosen for her. Mac was learning to ride on the same horse.

"I do," he said.

Not that it made any difference. Once February arrived, he'd have a child to support, and to do so, he'd need an income. The Wagging Tongue Ranch would have to carry on without him.

They rode for an hour before heading back to the house. The boys would be getting home from school any time now and Jake would come to the kitchen for coffee so he could sit with them for a few minutes before finishing chores. It was also time for Zack to start cooking supper, so for the next half hour, the family would all be together.

Luke unsaddled the horses before turning them loose in the paddock next to the barn with the others. Thunder, Mac's colt, trotted over to check out the new human. Mara rubbed his nose.

"I wish I'd thought to bring treats," she said.

"He's too young for that." Luke leaned on the rail so he

could relax and enjoy watching her. "He has to learn manners first. Feeding him treats teaches him to beg. Worse, it can teach him to bite. Only Mac gets to feed him, and even then, only when one of us supervises."

Mara crinkled her nose. "Ranchers are harsh."

Thunder, realizing he wasn't going to get more than a nose rub out of Mara, kicked up his heels and took off, bucking stiff-legged across the paddock. She laughed at his antics.

She liked it here. He'd hoped she would.

He heard the school bus clang to a stop at the end of the drive, then the groan of the doors as they popped open to spit the boys out.

He took Mara's hand, his daydreams dispersing. "Let's go get a coffee."

"Hi, Miss Ramos!" Finn shouted, spying her as he ran up the driveway, his book bag hanging off one shoulder to give him a lopsided gait. Mac followed more slowly behind him.

Finn dropped his book bag on the ground and struck a dance pose, his arms extended. He pivoted on one foot in what Luke could only guess was supposed to be a pirouette.

"Your form is excellent," Mara congratulated him.

Mac picked up Finn's bag on the way by and passed it back to his brother without comment.

They crowded into the kitchen. Jake entered a few moments behind them. He'd stopped in the laundry room to wash his hands and remove his coveralls. Zack had the coffeepot on. He'd also made sandwiches out of his homemade focaccia bread and roasted vegetables slathered in sun-dried tomato mayonnaise. Luke had dropped a hint about the bread. A search for fennel seeds was what had brought him and Mara together and he wondered if she'd remember.

Jake was the only one who'd never met her. He was also the family member whose opinion mattered to Luke the most. Jake froze for a second when he came into the room, almost as if he couldn't quite believe what he saw. Mara, all blue-eyed, Mayan goddess, who was listening to Finn chatter while she reacquainted herself with Lydia, had that effect on most men. His eyes tracked to Luke. His expression said, *"Seriously? What is a woman like that doing with you?"*

Luke didn't know, either. He simply chose to be grateful. But she was holding back on him, as if a part of her had shut off. She didn't trust him and he ached to prove he deserved it.

"It's nice to finally meet you," Jake said, shaking Mara's hand. "We've heard so much about you."

Funny, Jake.

That was his brother's idea of a joke. Luke had said very little about her, and she would know that. She knew him too well.

Mara, however, caught on to Jake's deadpan sense of humor. Her smile was all innocent sweetness. "I hope he said nice things. He's been very complimentary of you."

Score one for Mara. Now Jake was going to wonder exactly what she'd been told. It would drive him nuts.

Finn had finally wound down, letting them finish their coffee in peace, when a car door slammed in the yard. Zack, standing next to the counter, peered through the yellow curtains covering the window over the sink. The expression on his face shifted from curiosity, to unease, to alarm. He shot Luke a look filled with warning.

"Uh…" he said, as if that were a legit explanation.

Jake stood up to take a look, too.

"No idea who that is," he said, his disappointment apparent. He must have been hoping for Lacey, who'd still be at work.

But Luke had begun to get a bad feeling. Zack was sending out signals more appropriate for a pending apocalypse than a nosy neighbor dropping by to see what the family was up to.

The apocalypse knocked on the front door.

"I'll get it," Zack said. He twitched his head in the direction of the back of the house while making faces at Luke.

And Luke finally figured it out—but it was too late. Mara had, too. Jake was clearly confused, not that it mattered. In a few minutes, he'd find out all about it.

"Hello, Zack. Is Luke home?" Denise said.

Chapter Fourteen

DENISE HALTED AT the door to the kitchen. She took in the room at a glance. Her gaze settled on Mara, who, to her credit, remained serene and unruffled.

"I've come at a bad time," Denise said.

Mara stood. Her gaze on Denise was equally assessing. "Not at all. I was just leaving."

Jake and Zack looked at Luke. Jake was fitting the pieces together. Zack looked as if he were reaching for popcorn, prepared to enjoy the show, because why the hell not?

Luke scrambled to his feet. He couldn't say exactly what conclusions Mara had reached, but he did know he had about ten seconds to conduct damage control. "I'll walk you to your car."

The walk took forever.

Outside, by her car, Mara stopped. She reached in her jeans pocket and pulled out her keys.

"If you try to kiss me," she said, rounding on him with a smile on her face for the benefit of anyone who might be watching from the kitchen window, "I'll punch you."

He'd been about to, only because he hadn't known what else to do. "What—I look stupid to you?"

"At the moment, yes." Her smile softened. "I told you I'd be waiting for you and I meant it. The waiting begins. I trust you, Dr. Pretty."

She was the only person other than his immediate family who'd ever called him dumb to his face. He'd never loved her more than he did in this moment. She got in her car. The window was down.

"Thank you, *mi hermosa bailarina.*" *My beautiful dancer.* "I love you," he said. "Don't ever forget it."

She waved before driving off. She didn't, however, say she loved him, too.

He went back to the kitchen. The scene was awkward at best. Jake and Denise had never met. Zack had met her and didn't like her. He was now weighing his dislike against the fact she was about to be the mother of his next niece or nephew. The struggle was real.

Denise didn't deserve to be disliked simply because Luke had allowed himself to be convinced he wanted something that, deep down, he didn't. That was on him. He'd been caught up in academia and a career path that had seemed, on the surface, to be perfect for him.

Never again.

Mara saw him. The *real* him.

Was he being selfish?

"Hey," he said to Denise. "Last time you were here, you didn't get to see the anaerobic biomass power generator. Let me give you a tour."

Her heels, while practical enough under the right conditions, were meant more for the office or a classroom than a working ranch. He held her arm as they crossed the yard, then slid the heavy door to the generator room closed on its tracks. She wasn't interested in the technology, and the room was hot and noisy, but at least they were alone.

"How are you feeling?" He had a moment of panic. "Is everything okay with the baby?"

She wasn't quite four months along, but she was slightly built and the dress she wore did little to hide her condition. He wished so hard that things could have been different for them and their child, but time couldn't be reversed and there was no going back.

"The baby's fine."

"Then why are you here?" he asked. "Should you be traveling? I've offered to come to Seattle and go to your doctor's appointments with you."

Denise placed a hand on her belly. "I'm pregnant, not disabled. I have questions. I want answers."

He owed her this. Her life had taken an unexpected turn, too. They'd all have to adjust. "So ask."

"They aren't those kinds of questions. You're going to want to bring our baby here. I want to know what I'd be exposing him or her to. I needed to see for myself."

Now he got it. He sighed, rubbing the back of his neck. "Is this about Mara?"

"Of course it is." Denise folded her arms, hugging herself. "She's very beautiful."

"So are you."

"But it's not enough."

"No," Luke said. "It's not and never was. And it's not

about her, either. But you knew that already."

"I did. I just—"

The wide door slid open. Jake stood there, the setting sun at his back. "Sorry to interrupt," he said, not sounding sorry at all, "but Luke, can you spare a few minutes?"

Luke hadn't thought things could possibly get any worse, but he was wrong. Jake was about to go all big brother on him.

"I'd better take you back to the house," he said to Denise. "The last time Jake and I had a serious discussion, we exchanged black eyes and bloody noses."

A HALF HOUR later, he and Jake were locked in the study Luke used as an office.

Denise was in the kitchen with Zack, doing her best to fake an interest in Finn and Lydia. Mac had retreated to the paddock to hang with his horse, freaked out by all the tension. Just when he'd been doing so well…

What a great example Luke was setting for him.

"How the hell did you get yourself into this mess?" Jake asked. He didn't sound mad, more confused. "You're supposed to be smart."

Luke dragged both hands down his face. All he wanted to do was chase after Mara, to make sure she was okay, and didn't read anything she shouldn't into Denise's unexpected arrival, but he had to deal with one fire at a time.

So instead, he told his brother the whole story—how

Denise had walked out on him before the memorial service, and then he'd met Mara.

Jake leaned back in the leather chair. Luke could see his father sitting in the same position, wondering what punishment to mete out for the latest transgression teenaged Luke had committed. Luke had thought back then was rough.

Those were the good old days.

"You're throwing away a life with a woman you've known for five years, who you planned to marry and who's carrying your baby, for a dance instructor you met a few months ago," Jake said. "Have I about summed it all up?"

"The abstract never quite captures the essence of the entire paper," Luke said. "First I have to present my case, then summarize the actual results as compared to the initial expectations."

"So summarize them for me."

"Denise and I shared academic dreams, but my dreams changed and hers didn't. The plane crash made me realize it."

"That tells me about Denise. Now tell me about Mara."

"It wasn't anything serious at first. But then it was." Luke wasn't sure how to explain it. "She makes me feel," he said simply. "When I'm with her, I don't have to think about what I should do or the decisions I make. I just... I know what's right. And I know what I want."

Jake was nodding as if in complete understanding. "That leaves the baby. You planning to do the right thing?"

Did his own brother really believe he'd abandon a child? Is that what Jake thought of him? "It depends on what you think the right thing might be. I'm not planning to avoid my responsibilities, Jake. The baby is mine. It's going to have a father. And Denise will have my support. She knows that."

Jake's hard face relaxed, or at least, as much as it was able. "How does Mara feel about it?"

"I'm not sure how she feels," Luke admitted, "other than that the baby is the innocent party in all of this. She thinks I'll reconnect with Denise once the baby is born and forget all about her."

"Will you? Reconnect?"

"No," Luke said.

"So what will you do?"

"I'll go back to Seattle once a month to be there for Denise while she's pregnant. I'll help support her. I'll go back in February for good so I can be there for the baby. But I'll take Mara with me." He hoped, but Denise's arrival wasn't helping his case. "And I'm going to be the best damned father I can."

Jake sat for a long time, lost in thought, mulling everything over. "You say your dreams changed. If not for the baby, what life would you have wanted?"

Luke met his brother's eyes—so much like his own—and was honest. There was no harm in it now. "I wanted to come home to Grand for good. I wanted to keep my share of the ranch. I wanted to help build this place up for the next generation of McGregors to come."

"You can still do that," Jake said. "We can set your shares aside and work out an agreement with our lawyer for when you're ready and able to come home again."

They'd already been through this. Jake had poured the last eight or more years of his life into dragging the Wagging Tongue into the twenty-first century. "The ranch is yours."

"The ranch belongs to the McGregors. I'm only one in a long line of caretakers," Jake said. "Our father left you an opportunity to become a caretaker too, if you want. You do. So take it. We'll work something out."

"Do you really mean it?" Luke asked, not daring to hope. Luck hadn't been that kind to him, lately.

"Why wouldn't I mean it?" Jake asked, sounding truly bewildered and more than mildly insulted. "Do you really think I'm that much of a bastard?"

"No." Luke didn't think that at all. "I'm having a hard time getting my head around how generous you're being. I'm not sure I would be if I were in your position."

"Of course you would." Jake leaned on the desk and pried himself out of the chair. He wasn't quite as tall as Luke, but he had ten more years of muscle build-up on him. "I've got to get back to work. What do you plan to do about our unexpected house guest? Who, by the way, looks at Lydia and Finn with the same expression on her face that Zack gets when he has to change a loaded diaper. I don't think motherhood is going to come natural to her."

Neither did Luke. That was why he had to be there.

"Denise can stay in the west wing," he said. "I'll put her on a plane home tomorrow. I'm spending the night with Mara." He had his key back and he wasn't giving it up again. Ever.

Jake stopped before opening the door. He turned around

and leaned against it. "I'm curious. What if Denise wasn't pregnant right now? What if she had agreed to move to Grand with you and you'd never met Mara? How do you think things would have turned out between you?"

"If Denise moved to Grand and we got married, we'd be divorced within two years instead of five," Luke said.

Jake nodded.

He headed outdoors.

Luke went for the kitchen.

The kitchen was empty. The whole house was quiet. Luke stepped onto the front porch. Zack was playing catch with Finn. Lydia watched from her playpen, which she treated more as a prison. She shook the sides as if testing the bars, an intent pout on her face. If someone ever slipped her a file in a cake, they'd all be in trouble.

"Where's Denise?"

"Uh…" Zack said.

THE RINGING DOORBELL didn't surprise Mara. She'd wondered if Luke would be bold enough to let himself in. She had, however, assumed he'd text first.

She opened the door. It wasn't Luke.

Mara couldn't find words.

Denise was tall and slender, with short, dark blond hair. She carried an air of cool professionalism about her. She wore a loose-fitting dress that didn't quite hide the baby bump forming. Or maybe that was because Mara knew it was there. She looked like a scholar—a pregnant one—and someone Luke would have more in common with than he did with Mara.

The baby increased the number.

"May I come in?" Denise asked, so very polite.

"Of course." Thank God Mara hadn't gotten to the crying stage yet. She'd been feeling too sorry for Luke.

Denise stepped into the studio. Her gaze took in the entire room at a glance. Her expression told Mara nothing of her opinion.

"Is there somewhere we can sit and talk?"

Mara hesitated. The only comfortable space she had was her apartment. It was where she and Luke had spent long hours together. Taking Denise upstairs would turn it into something… tawdry. The word was one a former dance instructor had used to disdainfully describe a burlesque performance she'd seen in Las Vegas, and yet, it fit.

Because Mara felt tawdry standing next to this woman. Tasteless and cheap. What would Grand think of her, the other woman, when this story got out?

They'd rallied around her after Little Zee, but Luke was one of their own. Denise, so polished and educated—so smart—was perfect for him. The whole town would see it.

"Yes. Follow me."

Mara prayed her knee wouldn't choose now to give out. She could see herself falling and taking a pregnant woman down with her. Thankfully, they made it up the stairs without any mishaps.

"This is lovely," Denise said when she entered the

apartment. "I never would have guessed from the outside of the building."

She sounded sincere.

Mara led her to the living room area. Denise took a seat on the sofa. Mara chose the matching chair. Then, she waited. She hadn't instigated this conversation.

"I arrived at a bad time," Denise began. "But I knew if I called, Luke would try to discourage me from coming and I didn't want him to overthink it. There would be no reasoning with him then."

She knew Luke really well. Mara's heart sagged a little lower. That was exactly what he would have done.

"I didn't come here just to see him," Denise continued. "I wanted to meet you, too."

"Why?" Mara asked. What good could possibly come out of this?

"He left me for a dance instructor. I was curious."

"He didn't leave you for me," Mara said. "He says you left him." And she believed him. Nothing the other woman could say would change her mind about that.

"I didn't leave him." Denise looked at her folded hands. "But he didn't leave me for you, either. He left me for Grand. I knew what would happen when he told me he wanted to spend a year here. He wasn't coming back to Seattle." She met Mara's eyes. "I have a question for you."

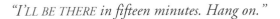

"I'LL BE THERE *in fifteen minutes. Hang on.*"

He hoped Mara could last that long. It wasn't that Denise was mean or evil. Far from it. But her cool rationality would have Mara convinced in no time that she was the reason Luke wouldn't return to Seattle tomorrow.

A response came before he got to his car.

"Stay right where you are. I can look after myself."

Luke had no idea what she meant by that.

"Does she have you at gunpoint?"

Two seconds later… *"Get over yourself."* She added a smiley emoji.

It didn't make Luke relax, exactly, but her next response did.

"We're fine. TTYL."

He played with Finn and Lydia while he waited for Mara to text him again.

Forty-five minutes later, Denise returned. Alone. She parked her rental behind Luke's car.

"I'm not staying," she said. "I have a room booked in town. I came to finish our talk."

Luke sent the kids to the kitchen with Zack, then rejoined Denise on the front steps. Night was beginning to settle in and she had a sweater wrapped around her.

"I don't want the baby," she said.

All of the blood in Luke's body fled to his organs, leaving his limbs too weak to support him. He crashed into one of the worn, thankfully sturdy, wooden planks.

"You're too far along for an abortion." He'd fight her on this, with everything he had. He'd sell his shares of the ranch to Weldon Scott, if he had to. He'd marry her, if that was what it took. That was what divorces were for.

And he'd hate her for the rest of his life for even considering the possibility. This was his baby, too. How dare she stand there and announce she didn't want it, as if he had no say?

"Calm down, Luke," Denise said. "I never said I want an abortion." She smoothed a hand over her stomach. Her gaze never wavered. "I want to give the baby to you."

LUKE GLANCED AT his watch. He'd had a little time before the gates to the cemetery closed, and while he wanted to see Mara, at the same time, he'd needed a few minutes alone. He'd wanted to talk to the two people who'd loved him from the day he was born, and who'd understand how he was feeling right now, because they'd loved each other, too.

If Mara didn't want this baby as much as he did, then they had no future together.

It would break his heart.

He let himself into the warehouse, then Mara's apartment, where she met him in the kitchen. She didn't throw herself into his arms as much slide into them, making herself right at home, where she belonged. He closed his eyes, enjoying the moment, wanting to hang on to it forever.

"She's not at all like I imagined," Mara said, tipping her head back to look up at him.

"How did you imagine her?"

"I don't really know. Less human."

Luke had to chuckle at that. "She's human. Very much so."

"She told me I was going to ruin your career. That I'd never be able to help you reach your full potential."

Thank you, Denise. "That sounds like something she'd say."

"Then she said if I make you happy, that's more than she's ever done."

That stung a bit. He hadn't made Denise happy, either. She believed her career was all that mattered to her, but she wasn't heartless, and someday, she'd meet the right man to prove her wrong—the way he'd met Mara.

"Anything else?" he asked.

"She asked me if I'd still want to be part of your life if you had sole custody of another woman's baby."

"What did you say?"

Mara reached up to cup his face. She pulled his head down so she could kiss him. It was sweet, and tender, and made him think of all the nights they'd spent together, and that maybe, just maybe, there'd be plenty more of them to come.

"I told her that if she was really wondering whether or not I'd love the baby as if it were my own then the answer is yes—although, it wouldn't matter because you'd never let someone into your life who couldn't love you both."

Relief welled inside him. She really did know him. "Do you love me?" he asked. "You've never said so."

"I couldn't say it. Now I can."

He knew her, too. She hadn't said the words to him because she was afraid he'd leave her behind. If she didn't admit to it, then it wouldn't hurt.

The pop star had done quite the number on her.

"I'd really like to hear them," Luke said.

She draped her arms around his neck. She hung her head back. The tip of her long ponytail tickled the forearm he had locked firmly around her waist. Someday, they'd have babies with eyes the same shade of blue as hers. They'd be dancers.

They'd be whatever the hell they wanted to be. He was placing no expectations on them. They'd choose the path they wanted in life. It had taken him too long to get here, to Grand, with the woman meant only for him in his arms, to stand in anyone's way.

"I love you," Mara said, soft joy in her eyes.

There it was. The look she'd had on her face when she danced in the video. The one he'd hoped she'd wear for him. And now she did. He'd never known happiness like this, before.

"What if she changes her mind?" Mara asked.

"She won't."

Denise would have thought it through before ever making her final decision. She wasn't ready to be a mother and might never be. When Luke thought of what her alternatives had been when faced with an unwanted pregnancy, and what his legal rights were, he chose to be grateful rather than question why.

"No," Mara said slowly. "I don't believe she will, either."

"Are you sure you still want me now that I come with a baby?" he asked. He had to be certain. "Do you think we can do this? That we shouldn't worry about the future and just let it happen?"

"Yes." There was no hesitation. "I love you. I'll love you both." Her eyes widened. He watched reality settle in, followed slowly by wonder. "I'm going to be a mother."

"And you're going to be fantastic at it," Luke said.

Epilogue

LUKE SHUCKED OUT of his tuxedo jacket and tossed it over a stool in Mara's kitchen, then loosened his tie.

He gave her credit. She had tried to prepare him for her family, but reality defied all description. His head was still spinning. It drummed home why she'd downplayed what an asshole Little Zee was. His fans would notice if he suddenly went missing.

Mara's father seemed decent enough. He did give off a drug lord vibe though, despite Mara's reassurances that he was nothing of the sort. And Luke was also confident that one of her cousins, not knowing Luke spoke the language, had threatened his life if he ever made Mara unhappy. Then her mother had sat him down and informed him that she was prepared to welcome him into the family, but he was left with the distinct impression that his welcome came with conditions and he'd have to earn his position.

Fortunately, Luke had women of his own to defend him. His aunts from both sides of the family—his parents only had sisters—had flown in from three separate states for the wedding. They'd loved Mara on sight, which had gone over well with the Ramos clan, who worshipped her as if she really were the Mayan goddess she resembled.

From that point on, everything had gone off without a hitch. They'd held the wedding at the Wagging Tongue Ranch—hardly the first one it had seen in its two hundred plus years, and unlikely the last, because big things were happening on the business front. The McGregors had plans.

Lacey, Posey, and Diana had been bridesmaids. Jake was the best man, while Zack and Mac were ushers. Finn and Lydia were ring bearer and flower girl, and thankfully, the mother of the bride had stepped up to take them in hand.

The reception had carried on into the wee hours of the morning.

Now, the three of them were exhausted. Mara, wearing a white wedding dress with a lace bodice that had to be glued on, because he couldn't imagine how else it stayed in place, refused to put the baby down. The newest McGregor, Orlando Xavier, wearing the tiniest tuxedo Luke had ever seen, drooled all over her bare shoulder, his tiny, puckered face pressed into the warmth of her skin while he slept.

Luke had suggested naming him Charles Xavier, after an X-Men character from Marvel comics, to see how Mara would react. She'd said fine, he could have half of the naming privileges, as long as she got to name him after Orlando Bloom, an actor from *Lord of the Rings*.

Luke had brought Lando home to Grand from Seattle a few days after his birth, and he wasn't quite a month old yet. They'd allowed Denise time to change her mind about giving him up, but she hadn't, and the adoption papers had been signed that morning, only a few hours prior to the wedding.

Mara looked so incredibly beautiful, with her hair pinned in curls that cascaded down her back and his baby—now officially theirs—in her arms, that he couldn't breathe. Less than a year ago, his life had seemed such a disaster. Now, he was the happiest man on the face of the planet.

"I owe you a honeymoon," he said, for the fiftieth time. He felt so guilty about that, but traveling with a newborn required a daunting amount of luggage and they weren't about to leave Lando behind. Instead, they were spending the weekend in the loft apartment, truly alone for the first time as a family.

She lifted her gaze from the baby, her blue eyes meeting his. Joy filled her expression…

And there it was again. The soft, dreamy look that made him love her so hard, someday his heart might explode.

She leaned toward Luke, one hand holding the baby's head, the other his tuxedo-clad bottom, and pressed a kiss to his lips that made him think that maybe he wasn't so tired, after all.

"I love you. I don't need a honeymoon," she said. "I have everything I want, right here in this room."

Luke pried Lando from her arms and tucked him into the bassinet she'd prepared for him under the living room window. He picked up the remote from the glass coffee table and flicked a button. Quiet music filled the air, but Lando, down for the count for the next few hours at least, didn't stir.

Luke held his hand out to Mara. "May I have this dance, Mrs. McGregor?"

She placed her fingers in his. The room glowed with her presence. She'd always be center stage in his life.

"Forever, Dr. Pretty," she said.

The End

If you enjoyed this book, please leave a review at your favorite online retailer! Even if it's just a sentence or two it makes all the difference.

Thanks for reading *The Rancher's Secret Love* by Paula Altenburg!

Discover your next romance at TulePublishing.com.

TULE
PUBLISHING

The Montana McGregor Brothers series

Book 1: *The Rancher Takes a Family*

Book 2: *The Rancher's Secret Love*

Book 3: Coming soon

Available now at your favorite online retailer!

About the Author

Paula Altenburg lives in rural Nova Scotia, Canada, with her husband and two sons. Once a manager in the aerospace industry, she now enjoys working from home and writing fulltime. Paula writes fantasy and paranormal romance, as well as short contemporary romance.

Thank you for reading

The Rancher's Secret Love

If you enjoyed this book, you can find more from all our great authors at TulePublishing.com, or from your favorite online retailer.

TULE
PUBLISHING

Made in the USA
Middletown, DE
22 August 2019